WRANGLING WANDA

BROTHERHOOD PROTECTORS WORLD

HEATHER LONG

Twisted Page Press LLC

BROTHERHOOD PROTECTORS

ORIGINAL SERIES BY ELLE JAMES

Brotherhood Protectors Series
Montana SEAL (#1)
Bride Protector SEAL (#2)
Montana D-Force (#3)
Cowboy D-Force (#4)
Montana Ranger (#5)
Montana Dog Soldier (#6)
Montana SEAL Daddy (#7)
Montana Ranger's Wedding Vow (#8)
Montana SEAL Undercover Daddy (#9)
Cape Cod SEAL Rescue (#10)
Montana SEAL Friendly Fire (#11)
Montana SEAL's Bride (#12)
Montana Rescue
Hot SEAL, Salty Dog

SERIES SO FAR

Securing Arizona
Chasing Katie
Guarding Gertrude
Protecting Pilar
Wrangling Wanda
Shielding Shayna
Covering Coco

ABOUT WRANGLING WANDA

No one taught him how to disarm his heart...

Clayton "Brick" Wall specialized in explosive ordinance removal, but a near miss, which almost cost his team their lives, left his nerves shot and his spirit a little broken. Even with his trusted buddy Hondo at his side, medical discharge feels like just another test he didn't study for—what the hell is civilian life anyway? A friend sends him to Montana to heal and the Brotherhood Protectors give him a place, and a purpose.

No one taught her to stay over the safety net...

Ex-CIA asset, Wanda Aiken is working overtime to keep her grandfather's Merry Circus afloat. Coming back had never been a part of the plan, but she's burnt on operations and family is family. When a series of accidents threaten to sideline the whole operation, she's torn between going old school, and throwing in the towel.

No one taught them how to not go it alone...

Sent to protect Wanda, Brick's not prepared for the stubborn, infuriating woman determined to do it her way. All he needs is one foot to get in the center ring. Fortunately Hondo has four paws and Wanda's charmed by him.

NOTE FROM THE AUTHOR

As always, thank you Elle James for letting me play with your characters. I have so much fun visiting Montana in these books I want to take a trip for real each time! Also, dear readers, some of the characters appearing here have shown up in previous installments. Sometimes, these guys just want to play their part. Every hero is different and the same can be said of the women they meet. How they overcome the challenges facing them, that's the important part...also, Hondo is probably my favorite character to date!

xoxo

Heather

CHAPTER 1

MUD SQUELCHING BENEATH HER BOOTS, Wanda Aiken strode through the fairgrounds. Snow clung to some areas, but the promise of warmer temperatures should melt it before they opened in three days. The fairgrounds were littered with vehicles off-loading, roustabouts hauling, and an annoyed layout man.

"Maybe we can move the midway," Roger said into his handheld.

"No," Wanda answered, dialing down the volume on hers once her voice would do. Roger pivoted to face her. "We need it to be within easy range of the food stalls and the Big

Top. Make them walk too far, and parents won't be persuaded by their kids to go…"

"Yeah, yeah I know." Roger squinted up at her from his mighty three and half foot height, then stuffed his cigar back between his teeth. He sucked in a noisy breath, then exhaled a waft of tobacco scented smoke. The man was a living cliché, but she didn't have a hope in hell of pulling this off without him. "I've been setting up since before you were a twinkle in your momma's eye, brat."

And the only man alive allowed to refer to her with that term, even if she could punt him. "Then what's the problem?"

She hadn't stalked across the heavily mudded ground for her health. If anything, she had to go over all the paperwork, make sure all the fees and licenses were up to date. That was the brighter part of the morning. Lunch with some auxiliary club providing volunteers and collecting a portion of the purse for charity was in her future. If it were at all practical, she'd rather be somewhere in Eastern Europe —having her nails pulled out.

"Problem?" Roger squinted at her. No she hadn't sprouted a second head, he was just in a mood. The layout man liked to control the conversation whether he was actually in charge or not. His nose had been bent since the announcement she would be handling this tour of the Merry Circus.

Folding her arms, Wanda counted to one hundred using three different languages. Practice kept her expression mildly pleasant as she lifted her eyebrows. "Not at all." Thankfully, she lied with such effortless ease she should be able to put it on her resume. Oh wait, she didn't want the jobs that came with those lies. "What did you need?"

One corner of his mouth curved while he kept that filthy cigar in place. Squinting up at her like some mad Rumpelstiltskin, he exhaled another cloud of noxious smoke before he tapped his walkie-talkie and said, "Put the midway closer to the big top, go pick up straw if necessary. We're in the middle of fucking Montana, there are ranches, go buy some from the ranches." He liked to do that, answer questions before they were even posed and cursing alongside those answers as if the other were an idiot for asking in the first place.

Uncle Roger was as much a part of the

circus as she'd been, she'd grown up under the supervision of his evil eye and foul-mouthed ways. He might play benevolent dwarf for the audience, but he was an asshole through and through.

He was also the best damn layout man in the business.

Wanda exhaled slowly. No sense in yelling at him. The man possessed demonic abilities to get under a person's skin, hers in particular but she'd seen him drive others to reaching for alcohol before dealing with him. So far, that hadn't been an issue. *The tour is just getting started though...we have time.*

Lowering the radio, Roger jerked his head to the right. "Follow me." Then he set off imperiously, no doubt expecting her to follow without argument. She waited a petty beat, then followed. Her longer-legged stride caught up with him easily. They bypassed where the center ring would be and rounded toward the backyard. The animal pens were quiet but it was an hour after breakfast, they were probably napping. They'd been offloaded from their train cars before dawn, and the temperatures were much cooler than where they'd been wintering in Vegas.

Roger charged across the area, ignoring the various greetings tossed his way. Like Wanda, most of the performers were either setting up the backyard, helping with the big top or running errands. There were no easy jobs in the tour. Everyone pitched in whether it was the bearded lady working with the cooks to get meals ready for lunch or the strongman hauling supply trunks to the various trailers. Kasetti, their master of animals, would be with Frank, the circus vet, double checking every animal made the trip as healthy as they were when they were loaded.

The scouts would finish papering the town, then move on to the next location to start all over again. They'd followed a relatively regular route for decades. Her grandfather built the circus up from a family operation to a mud show to an international sensation before he finally retired to Las Vegas and a permanent location.

The mud show, a family tradition, still traveled the smaller routes, towns not likely to be visited by one of the larger circuses. As

Grandpa put it, the family had made their bones in the small show and tradition demanded the family maintain it.

Hopefully his plans included her perpetual bachelor brother finding a wife, because Wanda planned on having kids—never. Roger didn't slow his roll until he made it all the way to the props trailer. There he pointed to the door dripping with...

Exhaling, she gritted her teeth and flexed her jaw before asking, "Is this a joke? A prank? A way to needle me for touring overseas?" Because if so, painting *you're all dead* on the props trailer was going just a little far.

Even amidst the musky combination of animals, mud, and diesel fuel, there was a distinctly metallic hint to the damp, chilly air. Roger jerked the cigar out of the clamp of his teeth even as she took a step toward the vandalism. Unfortunately, she did know what blood smelled like.

"Have you done a head count on the animals?" It was the first question out of her mouth, even as her gut twisted. They were in Eagle Rock, Montana, not Berlin, Bucharest, Krakow, or Moscow.

6

"Animals are fine, brat. I checked them first thing. Kasetti's been with them since they offloaded. Jojo and Lettie were going to pull their knives for practice when they found this. I told them to leave it until we checked it out." Roger hadn't moved a step closer to the trailer though. "But I wasn't calling the sheriff until I talked to you."

The denim jacket she'd chosen suddenly felt too thin for the chill in her blood. Digging her hands into her pockets, she pulled out a pair of work gloves. "All our people accounted for?" It was a rhetorical question. Roger was an ass, but the circus was his people, too.

"Every one I could track down." But the advance team would be in Eagle Rock proper, not out here near the train tracks. Some of the cast would be in town, too. Even as prepared as they were, there was always some shopping to be done and the inevitable hookups, which felt like they had to take their extracurricular activities off site. Roger just sent someone to get straw if needed.

"So we're not all accounted for." She didn't have a lab to test the blood, and that meant a call to the sheriff.

Great.

"Quietly check on anyone you haven't spoken to directly, anyone besides Jojo and Lettie see this?"

"Nope. Didn't think it would be wise. You take care of the cops, I'll take care of the others." With another nod, he jammed his cigar back into place and stomped off leaving Wanda with the blood penned warning.

Once Roger was gone, she tugged the gloves on and pulled open the door. It wasn't locked. They didn't lock up when they were unpacking, they'd never really had a cause to secure it when everyone knew everyone else. The smell of blood didn't follow her inside. Using the flashlight app on her phone, she scanned the interior.

The packing was tight, every container in its spot. Still, she studied each spot for a disruption. There'd been vandalism on a couple of the train cars, she hadn't paid it much attention. What kid didn't enjoy the original spray paint fantasy now and again? The items they'd caught with the paint could be scrubbed. They'd had a sick elephant before leaving, but elected to let her sit out this tour and be treated.

Problematic and expected, but this was different.

Her first thoughts went to possible smuggling. Maybe it was too many years of actively working black ops for the CIA overseas, but she didn't trust surface appearances of anyone anywhere.

Opening the containers nearest the door, she found nothing out of place. The next hour she systematically went through the containers easily opened by someone in a hurry.

A conspicuously empty spot was in the top of one tucked at eye level just three feet from the door. Conspicuous in her opinion, because the other items included her gear and she'd packed it herself. It had been full.

She'd have to go through it all to see what had been taken, but for now, she tugged it out and hauled it from the trailer. Careful not to touch the bloody marks, she carried it away from the props trailer. Once it was secure, she'd call the sheriff.

Hers was the wrong circus to mess with —period.

HONDO HAD ALREADY LEAPT to his feet before Brick caught the sound of the truck on the drive. Sliding the hammer into his tool belt, he carried the tape measure with him toward the top of the stairs. The ranch house he currently resided in, The Arches, belonged to a friend's new wife. While Angel and Katie were off on an *adventure honeymoon, whatever the hell that is...* he was there, doing repairs.

He needed the space, and had the skills. It was a good trade. The truck out front looked familiar. Hondo glanced up at him, and took off like a shot when Brick motioned him ahead. The German shepherd was his companion, war buddy, and partner. They'd both received medical discharge, and they were both figuring out the next steps.

At the front door, Hondo waited patiently for him to open it. Then he trotted outside to greet Hank "Montana" Patterson. The retired Navy SEAL grinned as he slid out of the truck. His wife wasn't with him for this visit, though she'd joined him when they picked Brick and Hondo up at the airport.

"Civilian life has been too good to you," Brick said by way of greeting, and clasped hands with the other man. " Hondo stood next to Brick and waited for his greeting, too. Hank didn't disappoint, he gave the shepherd a firm scratch around the ears.

"Can't complain," Hank retorted with a chuckle, then jerked a thumb toward the truck. "Brought you the wood Angel ordered. You know, the guys and I can give you a hand. We told Angel back when this went down, we'd tackle the repairs."

"I know," Brick followed him around to the back. Together, they lifted out the first plank of wood. "I don't mind the house sitting repairs, it makes me feel useful." The last thing he wanted was to be alone with his thoughts. The nightmares were bad enough.

Hondo paced them as they offloaded, periodically pausing to scan the area before falling in with them. Some habits were hard to break. Hondo knew to watch his back, and even the faint limp where he favored his left hind leg didn't slow his attention.

"Better to stay busy, you know?" Brick continued as they returned to the truck. The interior of the house had been littered with gunfire in places, there were boards up over some of the windows, and he'd already scrubbed the walls clean, and painted over some bloodstains. Refreshing a house touched by violence was almost therapeutic and less like free loading off a friend.

Well, a friend of a friend, but he'd met Angel and later his then fiancée back in Virginia after Cannon went through some crap. Thankfully, Brick missed most of the action. The cold sweats thinking about the explosion that took out the other man's truck made him feel more like a coward than a SEAL.

"Glad to hear you say that, I have a favor to ask." Hank's easy grin didn't waver as he neatly boxed Brick in.

"Sure you do." Not that he would complain. As a former SEAL himself, Hank hadn't asked a lot of questions about Brick's mental or medical status. The only thing he'd done was tell him he wasn't alone, and to call if he needed anything. Angel mentioned the other man might have work for him, if he were up to it, and if he wasn't—that was cool, too.

They were on their way back to the truck,

the cold air leeching off the heat as fast as their movement could generate it. For Montana, the hints of snow on the ground, the cold temps, and the battle the grass waged to offer up fresh shoots of green was a sign spring was on the way. For a southern California boy like Brick, it was like being trapped in perpetual winter.

Either way, it beat the hell out of the jungles and the desert, so he'd take it. "What's up?" he asked when the other man didn't continue.

"You know Ned Wagner?" The off hand mention didn't fool Brick, Hank had developed a tone when he brought him up. Since his *retirement*, Hank had launched a private business—the Brotherhood Protectors.

"I know him." The less said about the hows and whys, the better. If Hank knew him at all, he'd understand.

"He called about an hour ago and asked me for a favor." The guarded statement spoke volumes.

"Now you want to ask me for a favor. Sort of." He rolled his head from side to side, the feel of his vertebrae popping an audible stress reliever even if it wasn't an actual one. Hondo brushed against his leg, the weight familiar and grounding. Brick was in Montana for a lot of reasons, not the least of which was steadying his nerves. Not wanting to leave Hank on the spot, Brick added, "I told you to let me know if I could help out."

Digging out bullet holes and repairing dry wall and doors made him feel useful, but it was also light work for a guy used to defusing bombs. Not that there was anything wrong with light work. He was really okay with taking it easy.

"You sure?" Hank paused at the truck and studied him. Not insulted in the least, Brick waited him out. He'd made no secret of why he'd come to Eagle Rock, and he wasn't pretending everything was all right. Life, however, went on. He had plenty of opportunities—friends in Texas who were slowly but surely turning their ranch into a place where vets could get equine therapy. Eagle Rock had something similar. Another place in Texas had a full medical facility situation—and housing for those who needed a place to get on their feet.

He was blessed. He had backup and he had Hondo.

"I'm sure," he said, wiping his hands on his jeans. "I'm not made out of glass, and I'm not going to break. I just need to heal. Sometimes, healing hurts."

"Fair enough," Hank said after a moment, then he glanced at Hondo. As if aware that he too was under scrutiny, the German shepherd cocked his head to return Hank's stare.

"Don't worry about Hondo, he's as healed as he's going to get. We trained together, and worked the field together. If that bullet hadn't clipped his hip, they may not have let me take him with me when I was discharged." Fortunately, his application had been approved. He and Hondo had done a lot of missions together, and the dog was the best backup a man could ask for.

"I'm not worried, but does he ever sit?"

"When he wants to," Brick laughed. "But not when he thinks we're working." Which they had been. "He only sits then if he smells a bomb."

Hank blew out a slow whistle. "Good to know."

"At ease," Brick said, leaning against the truck and Hondo dropped to sit next to him, never losing contact. They called dogs man's best friend, and Hondo was all that an more. "So we're both good. What do you need?"

"How do you feel about the circus?"

Nope. Not what he was expecting. "I'm good with anything except clowns."

Clowns were creepy.

CHAPTER 2

"No, Ned, that's not how this works." Wanda kept her tone civil, even if her knee jerk reaction had been to just hang the damn phone up. Lieutenant Commander Ned Wagner, Naval Intelligence was a real pain in her ass. "You owe *me* a favor, not the other way around. So why are you bothering me?"

The sheriff and two deputies were combing the trailer. From a dozen feet away, Wanda kept an eye on them while keeping her distance. Dealing with local leos hadn't fallen into her job description when she'd been overseas. Hell, she'd almost talked herself out of even contacting the sheriff when a small fire had broken out.

17

Fortunately, no one had been hurt. The stink of smoke in the air made her nose itch. Two of the smaller tents had been damaged, and while frustrating, their loss wasn't enough to shut down the show. Roger was already in the process of rearranging the performance layout and getting the collapsible stand set up inside the big top.

Mentally she reminded herself this wasn't the worst problem she'd ever faced. However it was comparing apples to oranges to liken damage to her family's circus to any challenge she'd undertaken for the CIA.

"Wanda, are you even listening to me?" Ned's aggrieved voice reminded her he was on the phone.

"No, I'm not."

"You haven't even heard what I want." Damn, it was a good thing he was pretty.

"I think you need to introduce your upper lip to your lower lip, and shut up." After grinning briefly, she took a long drink from her coffee. "I'm out. Fini. Done. Think of me as pushing up daisies, if it helps."

"Why the hell would thinking of you dead help?"

"Neddy boy, I didn't think you cared. Or let me rephrase that, I don't care if you do. I put in my papers. I'm retired, lose my phone number." No matter how vehement she was, she kept her voice low. Sound had a way of carrying in the open space, and no one gossiped like carnies.

"Even for an old friend? That's kinda harsh."

"We weren't that close." It was time to end the conversation. No matter how she phrased it, Ned wasn't likely to take no for an answer. It was his job to get her to say yes, she understood that part. It was nothing personal. It was business. Except, personally she didn't want anything to do with that business anymore. Hell she barely wanted anything to do with the circus, and if it wasn't for her family and what her grandfather needed, she wouldn't be here either.

"Still harsh." His amusement told her she wasn't being harsh enough. "Do you think I could talk to less sarcastic Wanda for a moment?"

"If you want to talk to less sarcastic Wanda, be less stupid. I got work to do Ned, don't call me and I don't plan to call you. Later." She ended the call as the sheriff glanced in her direction. He did not look happy. Well that made two of them.

Her phone buzzed with a new call, but she recognized the blocked number. And she'd already answered once, so shame on her. Declining the call, she slid the phone into do not disturb then put it in her back pocket.

Wanda planned to be as cooperative with the local law enforcement as she could be, her people had to come first. Frankly the whole thing looked like a prank to her — just like the graffiti. Even the ill animal could be put down to normal course of events; the elephant wasn't the first one to get sick and wouldn't be the last. As an organization, the Merry Circus put the welfare of their animals first. That was why the elephant was back in Vegas. Fires happened, too. Also not her first and likely not the last.

Individually, all par for the course when it came to running a circus on the road. Yet all of these occurred in rapid succession over the course of five days? The damaging fire having happened mere hours after noticing the blood on the trailer door? Coincidence only stretched so far, and furthermore Wanda didn't believe in coincidence.

"They find anything yet?" Baz's familiar voice reminded her to put her game face back on. Former Naval intelligence himself, Baz retired a few years after she had gotten started. That fact the only reason he was with the troupe, was the last favor she had done Ned.

"Pretty sure the blood tested positive." She hadn't needed the sheriff to tell her that, she could read body language as well as the next person. Maybe even better. One thing her CIA recruiter had loved about her was all the years spent in the circus cultivated her ability to read an audience. Some audiences wanted funnier. Some wanted more daring. One thing they all had in common — they liked to be deceived.

"That's not creepy at all." His nonplussed tone suggested he expected nothing less. Not that she could blame them, she hadn't expected anything less either. "Roger's spinning a good yarn, but we'd be better off making sure everyone's aware there's a potential threat."

"No shit. I know everybody working for us, we don't have any new performers on this run."

Another plus, some circuses had a high turnover rate — the Merry Circus never had. People loved her family, and why shouldn't they? She loved her family. They were loyal. Straightforward. They made money, and remained successful in a climate where online entertainment had rapidly begun to outstrip the cost-effectiveness of the traveling show. Still, they didn't raise their prices nor did they change their style of doing things. They were familiar. They were entertaining.

Hopefully they'd still be here when the dust settled.

"As soon as I have something to tell them I will. For now, Roger is reminding everyone that we share responsibility in keeping an eye out. Kassetti and the vet aren't letting the animals out of their sight. I need you to spell them periodically make sure they eat and sleep. I'll do my time as well." They could replace tents. They could repair equipment. Losing one of the animals? It would be like losing one of her people. Unforgivable.

Dead calm existed in her gut. Maybe the call from Ned had been nothing, but couple that with all the other events — something was up.

"You got it. I need a favor."

What was it with people and favors today? Did she look like the goodwill fairy? "Depends on the favor."

"Don't be pissed. I made a few calls, and I got us some help."

Baz was damn good security all on his own, and when he'd said he needed to be out of town for a while and shown up on her doorstep in Vegas, she'd offered him a job. It didn't matter that Ned called ahead and told her Baz needed to disappear. At least in this case disappearing meant fade out of site not be buried in a ditch somewhere in the middle of nowhere. She'd had a couple of calls like that before — another reason she was no longer an asset of the CIA. All that said, she wasn't all that keen on taking on locals to be part of the crew.

"This is more than hammering a few nails and putting screws in the midway equipment." Besides the fact that there was already a potential threat plaguing them, did they really want to open the door to inviting the danger to come hang out?

Paranoia wasn't just a fragrance for men.

"Darlin' I was born in the morning but not this morning you know?"

Ugh. She hated old-timer speak and he damn well knew it. Still keeping an eye on the sheriff, she said, "We've had this conversation. Get to the part I'm not supposed to be pissed about." No she hadn't forgotten his caveat.

"I got us some help," he repeated his earlier statement. "Yes some of them are local, but all of them are skilled."

The careful phrasing didn't escape her. "What are they skilled at, Baz?"

"Come meet them, I think you'll like what they have to offer." Still not a direct answer.

"Baz?"

Breaking fingers through his steel gray hair, Baz shook his head. "You are going to have to lay down that chip on your shoulder one of these days before it throws your posture completely out of whack."

"My bones are made out of rubber or haven't you heard?" Undeterred by the good old boy act, she waited. Baz didn't want to give her a straight answer for fear she'd say no and leave it at that. Flicking a look toward the sheriff and his worried expression as he spoke on a cell phone, she had to wonder if the whole conversation was moot. If the sheriff decided they were too much trouble, he might yank their licenses and the spring tour would be over before they really got started.

"I've heard a lot of things, including your resistance to anything not going the way you have it planned. Give me a few minutes of trust to prove my guys can do more than just help us set up."

There it was. He'd hired some kind of protection. Dammit. "Who are they?"

"Come meet them." Unrelenting. Of course, Baz's unwavering determination was one of his finer qualities.

"Is Ned involved?" Her voice might've raised a fraction higher than she intended, but if she followed Baz out front and found Ned waiting with more of his Naval Intelligence and CIA liaison peeps on the hook, this was going to turn into an entirely different kind of conversation.

"I wouldn't do that to you." His voice changed, almost modulating an emotional response he didn't want to put on display. Respect for this man went a long way with her, but so did loyalty. She knew Baz was an old family friend for Ned, as well as Naval Intelligence. If he were this guarded discussing someone with those kind of emotional ties — she was better off leaving it alone.

"Let's go." If he suspected anything amiss with her giving in so easily after resisting the earlier offer, Baz didn't say anything. With one last look at the sheriff and his men, she nodded to one of the roustabouts who'd been sticking around close enough she knew Roger had told him to keep an eye on her. Catching his eyes she nodded towards the sheriff. Phil nodded. He'd linger in the area, maintain watch, and find her if needed.

Following Baz through the Big Top, she nodded to the crews still working. Gossip spread faster through a circus than it did in most places. They were their own small town, and what one knew, it was an easy bet so did a dozen others. The only way to keep a secret in a place like this was to tell no one. Like she had with Baz. She knew his history, but she hadn't told another soul. They saw him as the new guy, experienced in security and trusted by her. It was enough.

26

"Wanda," Baz said as he lead her toward four men who all screamed military. "This is Hank Patterson." The man in questioned straightened. His expression was polite and his green eyes cheerful enough. Didn't matter, she knew his name. Yeah, these were more than just some local help.

"Tate Parker." The man in question had dark hair, and dark eyes. He moved with an uneven cadence, favoring one leg over the other. Though not much, it was enough to notice. "Chris Kirkwood." The third man wore an unreadable expression, but he was as familiar to her as Ned Wagner.

They'd met before. Only, then he'd been Delta Force and went by the name Jammer. Filing the mental note away, she studied the last guy.

"And last, Clayton Wall." The fourth man hadn't drawn any attention at all, but he was as military as the first three. His dark blond hair ruffled in the breeze. Though not as high and tight as some military cuts, he couldn't have been out long enough for it to grow. The blue eyes though, they were the color of midnight and piercing. It was like seeing the deep blue of the sky first thing in the morning, before the sun could lighten it.

Setting aside the absurd poetry of that thought, she cut a look at the dog standing next to him. The German shepherd's ears cocked toward her, his mouth open and tongue peeking out. He wasn't panting or at all stressed, but he did maintain physical contact with Clayton.

"Wanda Aiken," she said before Baz could continue and offered her hand to Hank. He seemed to be leading the little expeditionary force. He gave her a quick, polite handshake and nodded. "Don't take this the wrong way... none of you look like locals needing a job."

Hank and Tate both grinned, but Jammer's expression didn't change. *Chris. Or Mr. Kirkwood.* Nicknames weren't that unusual, but he'd been introduced as Chris, she had to respect it. Clayton's expression didn't change either, but his posture did. He wasn't looking at her, but behind her. The dog cocked his head, his ears alternating between flicking back at Clayton then forward again.

"Sheriff," Hank called. "Good to see you."

"You too, Hank. Your guys on this job?"

Wanda pivoted, but the sheriff was already shaking Hank's hand. "That's the plan, but we'll leave it up to Miss Aiken. It's her place. Her rules."

"Yeah, keep an eye on them. The circus is popular and I'd sure hate to shut it down."

So would she.

The sheriff transferred his attention to her. "Miss Aiken, we'll be in touch. We've taken samples and documented the vandalism." Nice choice of words. "So you and your people are free to use the trailer again and clean it up if you like. Let me know if anything is missing, all right?" He glanced in the direction of the damaged tents.

Damn. The fact he added the question suggested he hadn't accepted her earlier evasion about the smoking heap. Accidents happened, and it was better to keep it that way. Smiling, she nodded. "Will do, Sheriff. Thank you. Free tickets for you and your men and your families on opening night."

"Appreciate that, ma'am." Then the sheriff left, and she found the four men watching her probably how she'd been watching the sheriff. No one spoke until after he was out of earshot.

29

"As I was saying…you gentlemen don't look like locals needing work." No amount of shoveled shit would convince her otherwise. So what were they doing here?

"Sorry Wanda," Baz said. "I pulled rank and called your grandfather. One act is a nuisance. Two a coincidence. After the fire though? Not risking it. He asked me to bring someone in to watch your back. Hank's local, and he can help."

"You did *what?*"

BRICK CAUGHT the 'back the fuck off' signals loud and clear. The woman was stunning to look at, and he'd have to be blind not to notice her. Tanned skin, light brown hair, butterscotch brown eyes, and pale pink lips—she looked like the girl who would seem local everywhere. Dressed in jeans, a blue jacket and work boots, she appeared pretty damn comfortable amidst the controlled chaos of the circus setting up.

Seriously, a circus. It would take time to wrap his mind around that. He didn't think he'd been to one in…ever. Hondo pressed against his leg, tail wagging once. The motion pulled his attention from the denim wearing goddess. When the sheriff seemed relieved to see them, though, a warning bell went off. Hank told him someone might be harassing the circus, and there had been a couple of accidents.

The less than warm, unwelcome wagon aside—the sheriff radiated concern. Then came the comment about her grandfather. Brick's issues aside, the whole thing had the stink of set-up. But what kind of set-up?

"The old man asked me to keep him in the loop." The revelation from Baz definitely wasn't winning them friends or influencing people. "Before you blow up, I did it so Roger wouldn't. It was tearing the guy up. He wanted to call him since he's still the senior shareholder in the circus and this is his baby."

Brick didn't know Wanda, but the chillier her expression grew the less impressed she seemed to be with Baz's explanation.

"I got him off the hook and called him—and..." he said, holding up a hand when her lips parted. "*And* all I told him was there had been a couple of vandalism incidents, and

Roger thought we might want to add security."

"That old fart probably said do it without telling Wanda, too." She ground the words out between her teeth, but despite the use of the words old fart, genuine affection colored the words.

"That he did. Ned told me about these folks." Whatever ground Baz gained, he lost with the last remark. "Said Trudi's boy Flint knows some of them."

"Well, Flint and Cannon are friends," Brick found himself saying. "Friends of friends, anyway." He knew them and had worked with them. Cannon was a crazy son of a bitch, but a damn good SEAL and an even better friend. Speaking up earned him a pinned glare from Wanda. What did it take to get on the woman's good side?

"Friends of friends...you're all military or ex—we don't have to play games. If Ned recommended you, then you're special ops." She faced Hank. "I know you by reputation, Mr. Patterson. I also know about the work you've been doing quietly, but efficiently."

"Eh, not always quietly." Tate chuckled, but

then the man had the nickname of Bear and his laughter came out almost a gruff, huffing sound. "We get the job done. We're also handy with repairs."

"Do you know the first damn thing about a circus?" Stiff tone aside, Wanda swept her gaze across them all before she focused on Brick again. He straightened under the scrutiny.

"Nope," he said, since she'd put him on the spot. "But I do know how to follow orders and directions. If you need a general handy man, I can do that. If you need someone to stand there and look forbidding, we can do that, too." Though playing watchdog wasn't his favorite assignment, he wanted to defuse any potential explosion on her part. She had every right to be pissed. Baz had gone around and over her head. "Look, we're here—put us to work."

Jammer shook his head. "Always trying to lighten the load, man." The words were softly spoken from the corner of his mouth, but Brick caught it.

Pursing her lips, Wanda blew out a breath then shook her head. They were close, but no sale. Hondo abandoned him at that point and wandered over to her. The dog had a sixth

33

sense about people, and Brick trusted his judgment. He liked most folks, but if the dog ever met someone he didn't like?

Brick would just shoot them and save everyone the trouble. Hondo didn't seem off put by her body language or her tone, instead he sat down next to her and leaned his head against her thigh. *Yeah bud, I'm pretty sure she's wired to go off any time now...* Except he hadn't told Hondo they were working, or put him back on guard since giving him the at east command.

"Seriously," Brick said, taking the lead when Hank glanced at him with raised eyebrows. It was Hank's operation, if he wanted Brick to take point on this one, fine. He'd told him he'd help out. "There has to be some crap jobs that go with set up. Jobs no one else wants to do which means they'll be put off until last or done so hastily, someone might miss something. Give us those jobs."

A snort from his left was the closest thing he'd heard to a laugh from Jammer in a while. Wanda, however, stared at Brick once more and she dropped her hand to Hondo's head and began to pet him. They didn't need Brick, he could have sent his partner to break the ice. Instead of pushing, he met her gaze squarely. Truth be told, Ned Wagner and he weren't tight, and he didn't owe the man anything more than he would another sailor.

"What could it hurt to have the extra help and security?"

Still scratching Hondo's head, she said, "How are they supposed to do that when you don't know who belongs and who doesn't?"

Fair assertion. Maybe. "Are you so certain it's not someone working for you doing this? Baz mentioned earlier incidences." Maybe Brick should back off, but she wasn't outright rejecting them anymore and the tension in her shoulders seemed to be easing. Of course, it could also be the fact Hondo had risen to his feet and wagged his tail, but wasn't walking away from her. The world narrowed down to the two of them, didn't seem to matter that Hank, Jammer, and Bear were there or the fact that Baz stood just to her right. "If you only had problems here? Then you're right. We may not be able to identify those who belong from those who don't—not immediately. You give us a run down on the crew, and picture IDs would be a start."

Though he didn't look at Baz, the older man had begun to nod.

"Let's say the problems came with you, then it's a bigger issue." Brick liked to see the whole picture when he could. It wasn't the bomb you could see that was the issue, though. It was the ones hidden in plain sight that you overlooked. "The way I see it, if it's just someone giving you a hard time, extra security should scare them off and you get some free labor. Win-win."

"It's not free, I'm sure we'll pay your security fees." The haughtiness in her tone was gone, but not the impatience. "Fine. I won't lie and say I want you here, but I try not to be an idiot on purpose. I don't want any of my people being hurt. Thank you, Mr. Patterson— I'm sure Baz can get you all started."

Just like that, they were in and she was walking away. Brick didn't bother to hide his smile, particularly since she was taking his dog with her and she couldn't see his face.

"I'm going to go with her," he told Hank.

"You do that." Grudging humor in every word, Hank waved him off as Brick spread his hands wide, then jogged to catch up to the striding Wanda and Hondo the traitor.

Just inside the big tented arena, he paused when he found her pivoted and waiting. Hondo sat down again. Yep, she was definitely armed and dangerous. "Why are you following me?"

Direct, too. "You're right. We don't know the circus, you do. It's probably better if you have one of us with you or at least in sight." He held up one finger, then added a second. "Also, my dog followed you."

The corners of her lips twitched. Damn, was he about to get a smile? It vanished before making a full appearance. Damn. "I doubt either of you are going to follow me up there." She pointed upward. Tracking his gaze to where she indicated, he did a gut check.

"Why are you going up there?"

"Watch and learn..." Then she glanced down at the dog. "Sweet dog."

Well, since she gave him the order, he folded his arms and watched her sweet ass walk away from him. No—that wasn't walking away. That was a saunter.

Glancing at Hondo, he found the German

shepherd following her with his gaze and tongue hanging out. Yeah, like he said, he and his dog were in sync. When he checked on Wanda again, she was stripping out of her jacket, and then her jeans.

What the hell...?

CHAPTER 3

STRIPPING at the base of the ladder leading up to the wire was probably not Wanda's kindest act. Clayton and the others were there to help, and they were more than qualified to do the job. Jammer could probably do it alone. She'd seen him in action one horrifying weekend in Turkey. Based on what she knew of his reputation, so could Hank Patterson. Considering the company he kept, would Clayton be much different?

The bodysuit she wore below her clothes was hardly revealing or warm. They'd gotten most of the high wire equipment up. The line tension needed testing if nothing else, besides, she wanted to think and there were far too many people on the ground up to and including her new "protectors."

Flipping open a bag hanging at the base of the ladder, she pulled out a pair of nylon slippers to protect her feet then began her ascent. At the top, she stretched. Practice would loosen her up. This high, the body needed discipline and focus to achieve balance and action across the narrow wire separating the two platforms.

Wanda had been walking wires since she was old enough to walk. Though she didn't remember it precisely, her parents had dozens of pictures of her balancing in her father's hand and her grandfather's as they walked around. Closing her eyes, she reached her hands to the ceiling then brought them down. Her props had been in the chest she removed from the trailer-slash-crime scene. Without time to go through them, she'd left them secured.

Her first routines on the high wire hadn't involved anything more than her own skill and some music. Today it would be she alone with her skill and the audience of two—man and canine—below. Inhaling slowly, she schooled her thoughts. Ruthlessly pruning away everything but the facts.

Ill elephant, not really suspicious.

Vandalized train cars—possibly, but just as likely a random act.

Bloody message of *you're all dead* on the trailer door—definitely suspect.

Tent fires—possibly accidental, but in the face of everything else?

Wanda opened her eyes and took the measure of the wire strung between the platforms. As she breathed, she exhaled her frustrations and worries. She dispelled the nascent fears which cropped up thinking about her grandfather's cancer. Eradicated the worry associated with an attack on her circus. Targeted or not, if someone came after her people they were coming after her.

With a step forward, she tested her weight on the wire and then stepped back. An elongation of her arms, stretching her muscles, then relaxing them again. Each move a part of the choreography that not only let her mind drop into the state she needed to walk the wire but also warm up her core and remind her muscles they knew what to do.

Fearless, she'd been labeled her whole life. Without trepidation or inhabitation, Whirling Wanda dazzled audiences from the moment she entered the ring.

What a pile of elephant manure.

Letting go of the fresh irritation, she chose a song from the playlist in her mind and timed her movements to the music. Six steps out in a straight dancing stride across the wire, she concentrated her center of gravity to maintain her balance. At the center point, she went with a series of three step kicks before turning, perfectly into a modified plié. The motion was graceful, but as the music built, so did her speed and the playful flap of her knees before she pivoted into a turn and came up, arms high.

The buzz of information aggravating her faded as she gave into the dance on the wire. Returning to base, she increased her speed, and from the safety of the platform did a full pirouette before racing onto the wire again. She mirrored her extensions into a leaping pattern, though in truth she only took longer steps and used her arms as a counter balance.

Her work on the high wire earned her invitations to circuses around the world. Recruitment by the CIA utilized her as an asset in more countries than she cared to count. Most of the time, she merely picked up information and delivered it—breezing across borders as a performer. Other times, she'd provided cover to agents who needed access, allowing them to travel as her *lover*. All of it, though exhilarating in the beginning, began to take its toll.

A skywalk in Dubai to obtain necessary plans once. Another stolen moment in a foreign embassy. The work only got dirtier and more dangerous from there. Mid-leap through her fourth pass on the wire and sweat dampened her arms, but she was barely aware of the chill. The body suit would wick away the worst.

On her next pause on the platform, she locked into position and held. Ned Wagner calling the same day as vandalism and accidents plague the circus? Coincidence? Evil plot? Annoying fact?

Granted, her handler had been disappointed by her decision to return to stateside. However, they hadn't prevented her "retirement." Not even when she refused to agree to return in the event of a special assignment. Part of her success on the wire came from her commitment to the dance, and the movement. Her success with the company came from her commitment.

Once that began to waver, she knew she had to get out.

Midwire, she slid into the splits and dared another glance below. Only Clayton and his dog continued to watch her attentively. Neither had moved from their positions.

Curling her legs as part of the balance and dance, she gave the illusion of twisting even as she held her torso in perfect position. He hadn't tried to stop her, point to him. The dog was cute, another point. He hadn't freaked once to her knowledge—of course she hadn't gotten to her more challenging tricks yet. Still, three points wasn't bad.

Still, he knew Ned. Subtract one point. She was out and staying out. Life in the field had come close to burning her, and stars burned brightest before they went dark. One too many close calls and failing desire to continue —no, she was better off where she was. Satisfied, she did a rollover. The maneuver required absolute concentration and the second one more so as she gained her feet once more.

The wire tension was near perfect, giving her just enough lift to add bounce in her dance moves, but without rocking her stability. Another split, and she curved her legs on the wire so only her feet kept their grip, and then she rolled herself, curving around it. Her muscles were soft, and liquid. This was the part of the wire she craved, the part where it was all motion and the dance.

Weaving in and around the wire, it was like controlled flying while gamboling not on earth, but not in the heavens either. She was in a fleeting purgatory between letting go and...the wire snapped.

The sound whiplashed around her, and only registered as an after thought. A burn lanced her arm and another her leg, and then she fell. Exhaling, she hit the net and bounced. The impact hurt, but the pain would be fleeting. Bouncing once, she twisted and turned to grip the net and slow her momentum.

Lying there, she exhaled and then dared a look up. The perfectly tense wire hung in two pieces, glittering like a deadly garrote, which failed its task. No way it snapped on its own.

Just...no.

A scuff of shoe warned her of Clayton's approach, and she rolled off the net and onto quivering legs. A dribble of blood trailed down her arm. Meeting his gaze, she got her racing heart under control before saying, "Okay, maybe we do need you here."

The shepherd rubbed against her leg and only Clayton's hand cupping her elbow kept her from toppling. The adrenaline rush was wearing off and for all her fearlessness, the acrid taste of panic soured on her tongue.

They needed to double and triple check everything. And she needed to know who strung the wire. When she got her hands on the son of a bitch doing this, she might kill them herself.

It wasn't the threat of harm, but the damage to her trust in her people she resented.

"You looked damn good up there," Clayton said after a moment, and she locked gazes with those midnight blue eyes of his. "Impressed the shit out of me."

"Yeah?" For some reason, that alleviated some of her worry. Some. Not all.

"Oh yeah."

Needing her equilibrium like oxygen, she studied him. The hand on her arm was warm, the fingers firm against her flesh—but the grip was light, supporting and offering security. She didn't doubt for a moment he would release her. "How many points would you give the landing?"

The question sparked a hint of a smile to crease his cheeks. "The Russians would take away two points for the hint of a flail there at the end."

"Damn."

"But you get a perfect ten from me. Any landing you can walk away from is a good landing."

Wanda snorted. "I thought that was plane crashes."

"Plane crashes. Wire snapping. You came down. You survived." He dipped his chin and his gaze went to her arm. "You're also bleeding."

"And you were doing so well," she said with a chuckle, and pulled away. The quivering in her muscles and the hammer of her heart told her she was alive. Limping over to her gear, she added, "We're going to have to brainstorm a plan."

"Thought you'd never ask."

Sure he had.

Time to play the game one more time. They had a problem, a real one. She was good at ferreting problems out. Checking her arm, she grimaced. Between the laceration on her biceps and the one on her thigh, she was also going to need some really big Band-Aids.

"Tell me something Clayton—do you have a nickname?" Then she glanced at the dog. "And does he have a name?"

"Hondo."

Him or the dog?

Her confusion must have showed because Clayton grinned for real and her heart did an uncharacteristic twist. "My friends call me Brick."

Brick Wall. "Seriously?"

A nod was his only answer. "You?"

What the hell... "Whirling Wanda the wild funambulist, at your service." It was her turn to extend her arm first. When Brick clasped her hand, a jolt of electricity assaulted her system.

"I get where you got the name, partner."

Weird. She'd never really had one of those before. "I'll trust you can live up to yours, then."

His wink eased her more than anything else he'd done or said. Of course, it helped he was still holding her hand—or was she holding his? Either way, the connection was there.

Of all the places in the world to meet someone that interesting and it was in Eagle Rock. Life was strange.

Hondo bumped her and broke the staring spell holding them captive. Brick frowned, and then chuckled at his dog. "Hondo's right, let's get you patched up and then we'll get to work."

Work. Right.

They had a saboteur to catch.

THREE DAYS LATER...

WANDA WAS a tough nut to crack, but Brick had to admire how she handled their current situation. After the high wire incident, she embraced the presence of Hank's protectors. Oddly, Brick seemed to be the one she was most comfortable with, and thus he and Hondo took over her personal security.

After patching her wicked looking injuries, she went to work accompanied by Baz, and the gruff, cigar smoking dwarf Roger. Dwarf probably wasn't the most politically correct term, but the man couldn't be taller than four feet. Size, however, played little part in the thoroughness he applied to the task. They ordered a cease to all activities, and every item of equipment was to be gone over, checked for safety and then checked again by Wanda or the other two men. Their relentless safety checks netted two more damaged set pieces. Neither was critical, but their efforts redoubled at those discoveries.

The weather cooperated. A spring snowstorm struck, and gave them a rational reason to delay the opening. The sheriff also paid another visit. The blood on the trailer was human, and after an exhaustive search by all parties—no bodies turned up. Wanda kept her cool, to the point Brick had to wonder about her. No one was that calm.

Her circus friends were all on edge. The seemingly calm Baz's temper frayed and the permanently in a bad mood Roger seemed one cigar chomp away from erupting. His language grew increasingly colorful, and he snarled at nearly everyone he came into contact with save Wanda. With her, he modulated his tone—more paternal.

One thing they all had in common, they worried about Wanda. In fact, everyone worried about her—except her. Even now, kicked back on the sofa in her trailer with Hondo sprawled next to him, Wanda worked. The woman was a force of nature, always on the move. Even when she was absolutely still, he found himself holding his breath in antici-pation of her launching into the next activity and appreciating the strange irregularity of the rhythm they'd found.

Folding his arms across his chest, Brick let his eyes fall closed. Since she never stopped, he kept up with her. Sleeping in snatches of time here and there was bound to take its toll on both of them.

Between one breath and the next, he went from a restive moment to a sweaty field. *Back damp, he lay on the ground, working his knife carefully around the claymore. Of all the places he'd ever been, the jungle was his least favorite particularly when on a mission of drug interdiction. The gang of thugs they tracked had access to antiquated munitions to spare. Those were bad enough, as evidenced by the field he and his team happened into, if not for the way the light had bounced, they might all be in this field in pieces.*

Fucking claymores.

With steady nerves, he eased the dirt away from the edges. The whole area could be seeded with these...something stopped his knife and he shifted his weight to get a better look. Wires went off into the dirt.

Wires to a claymore.

Seeded and connected.

A click.

Time suspended. The sweat rolling down his face slowed, a drop hanging in mid-air. Disarming the device suddenly presented a fresh jeopardy if it were connected. Modified, buried in the jungle surrounded field, at the mercy of the humidity and the elements and the hope that whoever did it knew their job.

"Withdraw," he ordered into the radio. "As swiftly as possible."

He'd left Hondo with the team leader, and even as he issued the order, he was backtracking away from his location. A half dozen steps...it was as far as he made it when the clicking stopped and the exploding began.

Eyes jerking open, Brick became aware of Hondo's weight at his side and the quiet regard of the woman still working at the makeshift desk next to her bed. The trailer was small, but for the first time, it seemed claustrophobic. Sweat soaked his shirt, and he sat up slowly. The dream too close to the surface of what happened, only he'd been smarter in the dream.

Instead of saying anything, Wanda rose and passed him to step into the makeshift kitchenette. She handed him a bottle of water and some aspirin, then poured two cups of coffee. After passing him one of the cups, she returned to her desk. Hondo remained pressed against his leg. It was still dark outside, but she didn't look as if she'd even gone to sleep. At all.

Maybe he hadn't slept that long. It was possible. He couldn't control the dreams, or the reckoning with fear that followed. Crippling in the field where his brothers needed him to react swiftly and without prejudice. Impossible to overcome so far, and he wouldn't risk their lives to his flaw. After taking the aspirin and a long gulp of the extremely black, and ragingly strong coffee—he glanced at Wanda again. "What are you doing?"

His voice came out rough and his throat raw, as if he'd swallowed sandpaper instead of coffee. Another mouthful helped, so he finished the cup then started on the water. At least his hands weren't trembling...much.

"Waging war against the dark side."

Sinking his fingers into Hondo's coat, he batted her statement back and forth in his mind. "Darth Sidious dark side or Kylo Ren?" The difference being the former was cool, calm and deliberate in his madness while the latter was just batcrap crazy.

Leaning back in the chair, she focused her bloodshot eyes in his direction. "Damn, that's an epic nerd level question even for me." Then she squinted, as though giving the matter serious thought. "If I have to choose, I'd say Sidious. I'm not quite ready to smash every-thing around me."

54

At least she got the reference, and it pulled a smile from him. Still damp with sweat from the nightmare, he appreciated the levity. "Not crazy enough for Ren. Good to know."

Her laughter filled the room, the husky sound a sensual slap to his senses. The all to brief decadence ended before he could fully appreciate it, then she shook her head. "I don't want to open the circus to a disaster, I don't need to see any of my people get hurt. Thing is I can't figure out why someone would be trying to hurt the circus, what's the win?"

Crinkling the water bottle, Brick considered the question. "You don't own the circus directly, right?" He waited a beat for her nod. "And the whole thing is a family operation?" Another nod. "Any other circuses want your… what do you call it?"

"The tour?" Skepticism filtered into her expression. "Maybe our Vegas operation, it's pretty damn successful and we've got a permanent billet there. The mud shows? Those are just family tradition. We bring the Merry Circus to places that might not be a large enough draw for other shows. Hell, the last time I checked, we don't make money on these tours. We do good to break even."

Exhaustion wore at her, like it would with anyone trapped between a rock and a hard place. She rubbed the back of her beautiful, long neck. Everything about her was graceful; she'd dazzled him with the display on the high wire. Despite everything, she kept her head and focused on safety even above the investigation.

"Hard as it may be to think about, is there anyone in the circus itself that would want to see *you* fail?" He chose the phrasing carefully. No matter the circumstances, if someone challenged him with the idea it was one of his teammates behind any problems he had—well it wouldn't end pretty. Loyalty was a valuable commodity and from what he'd seen, she had it in spades.

"Honestly? That's what I've been sitting here trying not to think about for the last few hours." Turning the laptop, she showed him a spreadsheet with a lot of data filling the screen. "I know every person working for this circus, some of them I grew up with and others I met on my trips home. There's no one working with us on this trip who hasn't been attached for at least five years."

Draining the water bottle, he latched onto one of the facts she let slip. "Trips home? You don't work for the circus full time?"

The shift in her expression was subtle, but still there. Her eyes seemed to shutter and she focused on the screen as she turned it back to her. Hondo rubbed his head against Brick's knee before the shepherd crossed the room to bump his head to her side. She dropped a hand onto the dog almost automatically, and then scratched his head.

"Let's take him for a walk," he suggested, and stood. "We could probably both use a change of scenery."

"And I can check on the animals." As well as the rest of the camp, though she didn't say it. She didn't have to explain the restlessness. It was the calm before the storm, knowing a mission was coming and not being able to act until they had details. He totally got it.

Hondo seemed to appreciate the idea, waiting for the at the trailer door while they both pulled on boots and jackets. Then they were outside. Dark save for the strategically placed floodlights, the grounds were quiet. Light snow fell, the tiny flakes. The last gasp of winter's breath as it were.

They walked in companionable silence, but Brick kept his head on a swivel. An uneasy feeling had settled at the base of his spine. It refused to be ignored, so he went with his gut. Hank, Jammer, and Bear were taking rotations, but he trusted one of them was out there, watching.

Hondo ranged out from them, but not far as they made their way through the snow. "Why the high wire?" The silence was fine, but something in her withdrawal stuck with him. He wanted to earn her trust.

Why? He wasn't certain. Or at least not ready to admit it to himself.

"I've always had a thing for heights...and control." The last word rode a rueful note. "I grew up performing. You know how some kids go to dance classes or play baseball?"

Even in the half-light, her calm expression betrayed not even a hint of wistfulness. "Sure. I was one of those. Baseball. Basketball. Hockey when we lived somewhere with a team. Bouncing from duty assignment to duty assignment meant sports was the fastest way to make new friends. Most of them were Navy brats just like me." Make friends, hang out, play a few games—move on. It was the way of things.

"Well not me, I learned how to ride a show elephant when I was three. I participated in the shows by the time I was five. I did my first rope walk when I was ten, and high wire by the time I was thirteen."

His gut clenched. "Your parents let you endanger yourself?"

They walked through the warehouse where the animals had been stabled. The tigers barely looked up from their sleep, curled together. It was warmer in the building, but even the pair of elephants were sleeping. How weird was it to spend day in and day out with trained show animals? He'd done some wild things over the years, but this was a new one for him.

The vet glanced at them and waved as they passed through, but he didn't stop playing on his phone. Based on the way the light shifted on his face, it was probably some kind of game.

"Don't think for a minute I was coerced. I'd have been on the high wire far sooner if Mom and Dad had let me. They do a trapeze act, or they did. They retired from that a few years ago, now they handle the day to day in Vegas and keep an eye on Grandpa. My brother worked with the animals, and he spent years perfecting his clown."

Note to self, make sure to know which one of the creepy clowns is her brother. Did it have to be clowns?

"He's got a tour right now or he'd be here. I love performing—there's something freeing about dancing on the wire's edge, and weaving in and around it."

Some kids joke about running away with the circus. Wanda didn't have to, she'd grown into the part. On the far side of the enclosure, she stopped and faced him.

"I spent the last few years touring in Europe with another circus. It was a different kind of exposure, new audiences, and a chance to work with different acts." But she was still holding back, and he couldn't put his finger on how he knew. Maybe it was just Wanda herself, she was so self-possessed and carried herself with aplomb. Yet, he didn't think that was all there was to her, so how much was the act and how much was the woman? "I actually toyed with the idea of leaving the circus life all together, and I spent four years in college planning to do just that. I studied sociology and political science."

Surprise flooded him. "It didn't take?"

"Eh. Too well, maybe. But I had lots of skills and sometimes you just have to go with what you know."

College. Whatever happened occurred then. Peeling back the layers was like studying the intricacy inside a bomb. There was an elegance to building an explosive device, even the crude ones.

Defusing and understanding Wanda would take every ounce of his patience. "I didn't go to college," he told her, and trusted his instincts to follow that track. "I thought about it, even made plans. Figured a four year stint in the Navy, pay for school and do some good at the same time…"

"Didn't work out that way?"

No, he'd been tapped for the SEALs and the challenge had been too much to resist. "Ended up where I needed to be."

Her gaze fixed on his and the connection

he'd experienced when they shook hands that first day pulsed to life. "Me, too."

The air around him seemed to grow heavy and the world took a step back, leaving the two of them in their quiet bubble watching a pair of zebras doze. Without realizing it, he took a step toward her and she narrowed the distance.

An alarm sounded, the frantic ring of a bell. It started the zebras, and Hondo spun and barked. Wanda was already in motion and Brick had to hurry to keep up. They raced across the grounds toward the ruckus and the spout of flames near the trailers.

It was Wanda's trailer, and it was on fire.

They slid to a halt, and Brick grabbed her arm before she hurtled right into the flames. "I hate to say this, but I don't think the circus is the target."

Twisting to look at him and backlit by the flames, she blew out a breath. "Better me than them."

On that point, he'd disagree.

His job just got a whole lot harder, because he'd be damned if anyone was going to come after her.

Not without going through him first.

CHAPTER 4

THANKFULLY, they'd gotten the fire out before it spread from her trailer. The trailer, itself, was utterly destroyed along with her laptop, clothes, and what few personal items she'd brought with her. The props tote survived, but only because she'd stored it outside instead of in the trailer. With everything going on, she hadn't had a chance to sort through it.

Sick and out of sorts with it all, she'd accepted Clayton's suggestion to stay offsite. Baz and Roger assured her they were going to be beefing up security, and for the first time since the incidences began—she considered sending the whole circus home. Risking real disaster wasn't an option.

63

It wasn't until they were in the truck and driving away that it hit her. "You didn't tell anyone where we were going, did you?"

"Hank will know," Clayton said, his attention on the road. Hondo seated between them offered a kind of warm buffer. The dog hadn't left Clayton's side once as they pitched into the water line. They had hoses set up for just these kinds of emergencies, but she couldn't think of a time once in the last twenty years that the circus suffered such a devastating loss.

"Hank will, but no one else. You still think someone connected to the circus is involved." Anger should have been forthright within her. Though he hadn't come out and directly accused anyone, his actions spoke volumes. Instead of righteous and protective fury, defeat weighed upon her. Defeat and the stench of smoke. "It's not Roger. Or Baz."

"Baz is new to your circus. Not all that long ago he was in the D.C. area, and involved in a news story that nearly got several people killed. Now he's here."

Of course he had been. She nibbled at a hangnail.

"Baz is also retired naval intelligence with

deep ties," Clayton continued without a trace of judgment in his voice.

"I know," she finally answered, her gaze firmly on the dark landscape along their route. Pregnant silence filled the vehicle after her acknowledgment.

"If it's need to know," he said, finally. "I need to know."

"I want to say it's unconnected. The circus was just a place for Baz to lay low for a few months. He needed to fall off the radar." At least that was the impression Ned had given her. Of course, he would lie to her if he believed it necessary to achieve the end goals or, at the very least, not germane to why he asked her. "It was a favor for a friend...okay friend is pushing it." At the moment, she questioned everything.

"Ned Wagner."

"You know an awful lot about this." She dragged her gaze off the dark and looked around Hondo. The dashboard lights only partially illuminated his face. The shepherd gave her a kiss on the cheek, a light swipe. Running her fingers through his fur, she gave the dog a scratch just above his collar.

"I've been doing some research," Clayton admitted. "Hank and his guys began to deep dive everyone's backgrounds."

Of course they had.

"Including yours."

Sensing a reckoning, she waited.

"I also asked a friend to pull your records. You've got a scrubbed background check, a very thorough and squeaky-clean one. So which did you work for?"

"The circus." It wasn't a lie. She'd worked for several of them.

"Wanda," Clayton's voice dipped low and a shiver rolled across the surface of her skin. "Is it possible they didn't scrub you as thorough as it looks? Could someone from a life you didn't lead in a job you didn't do for an alphabet agency you won't admit, be gunning for you?"

Laughter spilled out of her at the absurdity of the question, and she shook her head. "If anyone from a mythical life that didn't happen on a continent where I worked for the circus, and didn't do any side jobs for anything resembling an alphabet agency were to come looking —I'd guess they'd be a lot more direct than bloody threats on a trailer door and a fire to drive me out of my trailer."

"I don't think it was to drive you out." No more sobering words had been spoken. "Everything was done to systematically destabilize the production and to throw you off guard—until tonight."

He turned onto a drive she hadn't noticed, and killed the lights as he slid to a stop and turned off the truck. Though there was no house in front of them, he sat, half-twisted and looking over his shoulder. Mirroring his position, she stared back at the dark road. He was waiting to see if someone followed them.

"The fire tonight was meant to kill me, wasn't it?" They could dance around it verbally all they wanted, but since the high wire snapped she'd wondered. She was the only one using the wire in her act. The only person likely to be hurt, was her. Traditionally when she performed, there was no net. It was only her own stubbornness that sent her up to practice after everything while the net was up.

If not...she'd have been a smear on the floor. Or at the very least, a series of broken bones in a hospital.

"I can't say for certain," Clayton answered, his gaze still pinned on the road behind them even though no headlights were visible. "But from what I saw, there had to have been an incendiary of some type. It went up too fast. It also wasn't planted inside your trailer or Hondo would have alerted us."

Hadn't the dog wanted to go outside? Tired waged war on her memory, though. "Well, that's a thoroughly disheartening thought."

"Sorry, but not sorry. We need to know who or what it is, it's the only way I'm going to keep you safe."

"Maybe I need to keep you and everyone else safe. I can disappear." She did have some weirdly useful skills.

Clayton's hand covered hers on Hondo. "I'd rather you didn't."

The weight of his fingers, and the warmth of them combined with the roughness of the callouses on his hands flooded her with some highly inappropriate thoughts and desire. Like what would it feel like if he were to run those work marked hands all over her?

"Adrenaline fueled couplings aren't always the best idea." They burned hot, but also burned fast. She'd rather there was something of her left when all was said and done.

"Maybe, but I'm not feeling the adrenaline rush at the moment." The blunt reply pulled another smile out of her. She'd endured her fair share of special ops guys, and agency men. They all talked a good game. While they might want a night in her bed, they were also already on the move, one foot out the door to the next assignment or op.

"Who are you Clayton Wall?"

"Call me Brick," he said softly and the invitation curled through her until the hairs on her arm stood up.

"Brick."

"Better," his grin almost audible in his voice. "I'm a Navy SEAL, Wanda. Retired, but I spent the better part of the last seven years giving everything I had to my country. I can't tell you about the operations, but I'm a decent guy. I've got my issues…you saw one tonight."

The nightmare. It had been Hondo who alerted her just before Brick woke. The dog had risen to lean against the man, his touch grounding him as it was doing right now. The soft sounds of Hondo's panting filled the interior of the cab, but Brick didn't release her hand and she wasn't pulling away.

"A friend of mine suggested I come to Montana, get away from everything. A lot of guys I've worked with over the years have retired, medically or just timed out."

Being a SEAL was brutal on the body and the mind. More failed out of BUD/S than made it through. She'd had to do some courses at FLETC and later on the Farm. She knew enough to be dangerous, and to not accept the challenge to become a full-fledged agent. At her core, she was a pacifist, dark side tendencies aside.

"Are you going to be all right?" She didn't ask him what happened. If he wanted to tell her, he would. But the man? She liked him. She wanted him to be okay.

"I will," he said, assurance thickening his voice. "That's the promise I make to myself everyday."

"That's why I got out." She skated the line of admitting to something she wasn't supposed to talk about. "I wasn't going to be okay if I kept going."

"It happens," he told her, and gave her hand a squeeze. "Did it work?"

"I don't know," she admitted ruefully. Behind them the road remained quiet and dark. "Someone just burned down my trailer, and I'm sitting in the dark wondering what the hell comes next."

"When I went for BUD/S I did it to see if I could survive the training. It's one thing to be tapped for it, it's an entire other thing to make it through." His voice rolled around her, enveloping her in his confidence. "I learned a lot about myself—I learned failure teaches. I learned to listen to my instincts. I learned to trust the man in front of me, behind me and beside me. I learned to be worthy of their trust."

Why was he telling her this?

"I learned what I needed to survive."

He started the truck, and left the lights off as he backed onto the road. Then he continued, and it as though they were a shadow moving amongst shadows. He'd taken them off road, and adjusted his vision to the dark. Now he avoided detection—all to make sure she was safe.

"And even if you can't see a bright side yet, Wanda," he murmured into the shroud around them. "I'll sit with you in the dark."

THE ROUTE he took to the Arches passed without incident. Driving without the headlights was dangerous, so he avoided speeding. Encountering no other vehicles, or animals, didn't mean they were out of the woods but he for one was happy to arrive back at the borrowed ranch house.

Jammer sent a message to his phone, a single word. "Clear."

After he decided on the plan, he clued Hank and the guys into where he was taking Wanda. They would provide support but hang back. Ideally, whomever was after her would get frustrated enough to make a stupid mistake—like come at him directly.

He'd appreciate a direct fight at this point. Just to make sure the woman accompanying remained safe.

"Nice place," she commented after he parked in the garage. He didn't want her in the open, but he kept the thought to himself.

"Belongs to a friend's…" Maybe they didn't need the pedigree. "Friend's place. I'm staying here for the time being, and trading some repairs for the free roof over my head."

"Sounds like good work if you can get it." Weariness marked every syllable and step.

As much as he would like to spend more time with her, he said, "Why don't you go upstairs, shower—I'll toss a couple of my shirts in your room and you can use those. I can wash what you have until we sort it all out tomorrow." Should he offer food? "I can even make a mean sandwich and leave it on the nightstand."

The woman pivoted to look at him, drop dead gorgeous even with the ashes smudged on her cheeks and the red veins in her blood shot eyes. "You're kind of perfect…any flaws I should know about?"

Hondo bypassed them both when they lingered in the kitchen. He went straight for his own food and water. "I'm the kind of guy who'll do anything he has to protect what's his, and what he promises to protect. Sometimes that means any means necessary. I'm also the guy who gets so focused on a task, he forgets to feed his dog."

Troubled frown easing, Wanda lifted her hand and then raised her eyebrows as she motioned to his face. After his nod of permission, she traced a finger lightly over his cheek. "You need a shower, too. And some rest. You've also got a cut."

"I'll take care of it," he assured her, then caught her hand and pressed a kiss to it. "Upstairs, first bedroom on the right. There's a bathroom attached, and fresh supplies in it."

It was a testament to her exhaustion that she squeezed his fingers and trudged up the stairs without a word of argument or complaint. More surprising though was Hondo. The shepherd gave him a long look, then trotted after her. *Watch her back buddy.*

In the kitchen, he put together a couple of ham and cheese sandwiches, nothing fancy but it would fill the hole. He contemplated coffee, but he wanted her to rest so he grabbed one of the water bottles from the fridge.

Upstairs, the sound of the water running told him she followed his suggestion. He jogged up the stairs. Hondo lying outside the bathroom door, his whole demeanor that of protector. Trusting his partner to keep an eye on her, he left the sandwich and water for her. Then he went for the shirts he offered. He left them for her as well, before heading to another bathroom and grabbing a fast shower for himself.

The post-shower two percent improved mood rule in effect, Brick made a pit-stop at the door to her room. Though the light was still on, Wanda lay on her side, damp hair on a towel laid over the pillow. Sound asleep, she didn't twitch as he slipped into the room and took the empty plate. Hondo had moved from guarding the bathroom door to guarding the bedroom door.

Meeting the dog's eyes, he nodded to him and Hondo set his head against his paws. Yep, he and the canine had the same idea. Keep Wanda safe. Turning the light off in the room, he flicked on a light in the hall. It would be enough for Wanda to see if she woke, but hopefully would let her sleep.

Downstairs, he found Jammer in the kitchen and his sandwich gone. "Come in," he murmured. "Help yourself."

The other man grunted, a glass on the table with a half-a-finger's worth of whiskey in it.

"I'm here to spell you out for a bit," Jammer spoke in a near monotone, his gaze on the wall calendar.

"I'm wired," Brick told him, pulling out the ingredients for another sandwich. Hunger didn't plague him, but he needed to eat while he had the opportunity. "Kind of like the night before an op."

He didn't have to say anything more, Jammer nodded.

"Not that I'm judging," Brick added conversationally. "Sun's coming up. You planning on drinking that whiskey?"

"Just the one drink. I'll still be in good shape."

Maybe. It wasn't that Brick didn't trust him, but drinking on the job wasn't always the best idea. Sandwich built, he checked the milk with a quick sniff before pouring a glass for himself. Leaning against the counter, Brick checked the height of the sun outside. It was still hidden behind trees and cloud cover, but the sky continued to be a play on the varying stages of gray tinged with hints of pink.

They didn't speak, and Jammer didn't drink. His gaze, however, hadn't wavered from the calendar. Glancing back at the dates hanging on the wall, Brick finished his sandwich. There was a date marked for a wedding —and all it said was elope. Angel and Katie had done that a couple of weeks prior. He'd been good to his word and said nothing. The couple wanted time to themselves, and considering how they'd met—Brick could appreciate the discretion particularly as they were on their delayed honeymoon this week, location undisclosed. It had something to do with Katie's performance schedule, but he hadn't been paying particular attention to that part.

Then a second notation on the calendar came into sharp relief. The date had been circled and all it said was ANGEL'S BDAY. Angel's birthday.

Son of a bitch. Tracking his gaze back to Jammer, he sighed. Jammer had been engaged to Angel's twin, a woman who'd died a few months before. The guys didn't talk about it, but they all knew.

Lacking the words, he crossed the room and gripped Jammer's shoulder. The operative nodded once "Go get some sleep, Brick. The lady is in safe hands and I'd rather keep watch."

He still hadn't touched the whiskey. Probably wouldn't. He'd poured the drink for her. Understanding was a bitter, two-edged sword.

"Thanks man."

Leaving him to his sorrow, Brick headed for the stairs. Life sucked all the way around. At the top of the stairs, he considered the open door to Wanda's room. They'd been not-sleeping in the same trailer for days. Then they'd had no choice.

"Brick?" Her soft voice carried out to the landing.

What the...? Crossing to the open door, he eyed Hondo who merely thumped his tail a couple of times. Stepping over the shepherd's guard position, he found Wanda resting on one elbow. "Why are you awake?" She'd been asleep when he went downstairs.

"I never sleep well in an unfamiliar bed. I heard you come get the plate earlier."

Well shit. He should have left well enough alone. Folding his arms, he studied her tousled damp hair and the lines of her athletic form where she curled in the bed. Crap, he'd meant to take her laundry downstairs for her. Whatever, he'd do it in the morning. If there were a little more light in the room, he'd get to see which of his two shirts she'd chosen. Kicking his brain out of the gutter, he said, "Kind of weird someone who travels so much can't sleep in an unfamiliar bed."

"You forget, I traveled with a family trailer, and then my own." There was a hint of a catch in her voice on the last. Her trailer was gone now. "So I always slept in my own bed, just the location changed."

When she curved her feet away and patted the bed, he perched on the edge. *Talking, not touching.* The refrain began to play in the back of his mind. Attraction wasn't a new sensation, he'd met plenty of attractive women over the years. Very few of them, however, became someone whose company he craved in such a short space of time.

Wanda was all of that and more.

"What about Europe? Did you take your own bed with you?"

Settling back against the pillow, she rolled onto her back. Hands folded against her abdomen, she lifted her shoulders in a half shrug. "Took me months to settle into the bunk

I earned there. Then it became a second home..."

"I can sleep anywhere. Snow. Desert." Jungle. His throat closed on the last and the word wouldn't come out. "Rest is vital to performance. Sometimes, you only have two hours. You take the sleep where you can find it."

"Even on ratty old sofas that can't possibly be comfortable." The teasing note softened her voice, tethering him. Such a simple thing, yet it kept him from following thoughts of the jungle to their logical, and oftentimes painful conclusion.

"The sofa wasn't so bad." Then because darkness beckoned honesty, he said. "The company was pretty good, too."

Another chuckle floated into the air. "Stop flirting with me. We're both too tired to do more than bat at each other right now."

"Right now, but that really sounded like a challenge." The remark earned him another challenge.

"Maybe it is—a challenge for both of us." Then the humor in her voice sobered. "But you're already fighting one of my battles, and you don't know enough about my past to involve yourself further."

"Stop making decisions for me, woman." He meant it. "I'm a grown man, I'll decide what decisions I need to make and what ones I don't."

When she sat up and reached out a hand, he took it. "I don't like relying on other people, especially when I can't be one hundred percent honest."

"I get work. I get oaths," he told her, squeezing her hand. "I've had enough assignments I can't share that I'd be a jackass and a hypocrite if I judged you for the same."

"Have you ever regretted making the choice that put you in harm's way? That made you— have to be secretive?"

Two shadows in the dark, the irony wasn't lost on him. "No." The answer fell from his lips without hesitation. "I've lost friends, good sailors, to the mission. I've been to hell, and paid the passage to get my ass back out again. Every job I've done, every one—I stepped up to do those jobs. You don't accidentally qualify in BUD/S and no one goes through that without the dedication to work the other side."

She was silent, but he could almost feel her unasked question in the air.

"Ask," he told her.

"The nightmare? Was that a one off or...?" She interlaced her fingers with his, a comfort and an invitation. "You don't have to tell me, but...but you had a moment this—hell I don't even know what time that was anymore?"

Just a few hours earlier, but he appreciated the sentiment. "The nightmares are the scars I live with. Some guys lose a finger, or walk with a limp...some lose limbs. Me. I lose sleep. Not really something I can complain about."

Hondo huffed a little and turned his head to stare at them.

"I think we're keeping him awake," Wanda said through smothered laughter, then she tugged his hand. "Come lie next to me. We can both pretend we're going to get some rest so he can sleep."

Yeah, they wouldn't fool the shepherd, but Brick sprawled next to her anyway. He wanted to be close, and she didn't release his hand.

"I have bad dreams, too." She confessed. "Most of the time they're dreams about all the things that could have gone wrong. This thing…this whatever the hell it is with the circus. It's worse."

"Because you feel powerless." He totally got that. "You're not, though."

"Feels pretty damn powerless right now. My people are still at the site, and I'm running away. Their lives are being threatened and I'm…flirting in the dark with a hot guy." The mattress depressed between them and suddenly Hondo settled his weight where he was touching them both.

"And his dog," Brick said as they both glanced down at the shepherd.

Wanda's laughter returned and he lifted their joined hands to press a kiss to her knuckles.

"I'm totally into your dog," she admitted. "That's why I want you to stick around."

"I'm okay with that," he said. "It gives me time to convince you I'm worth it, warts and all." Her humor was infectious, spreading through all the dry, and worn places in his soul like a spring breeze. Exhaling, he said, "I think we should talk about something really important."

"Oh?" Her tension earned him a baleful

look from Hondo, but Brick persisted.

"Do you know who Corporal Lee Duncan is?"

Silence. Then, she said, "No. Friend of yours?"

"Sort of…" He had to keep a straight face, which proved more difficult when she rolled onto her side then rested her head against his shoulder. He liked the way she fit against him and didn't mind Hondo sharing the bed, too. "He rescued a litter of puppies in France, during World War I. Liberated them, you might say. Brought them home and trained them. One of those puppies went on to become Rin Tin Tin."

"Really?" Skepticism punctuated her tone and he had to bite back another smile.

"Rin Tin Tin was my hero growing up."

Hondo huffed.

"Brick?"

"Yes, Wanda?"

"You're crazy."

"Thank you for noticing," he said, utterly unrepentant. "Anyway, the corporal trained dogs for decades, most of his family does. Rin Tin Tin and all of his descendants. Then he trained more for World War II, and those dogs were some of the first to go into battle with us..." And he kept talking, telling her canine stories and eventually, her breathing evened out and Hondo settled.

Outside, the sun kept rising steadily, but Brick was happy right where he was—in the shadows with Wanda.

CHAPTER 5

EYES OPEN, Wanda stared at the unfamiliar ceiling. The night before trickled in, as did the sound of someone breathing right next to her. Turning her head, she studied the slumbering Brick next to her. His relaxed face made her smile. Stubble decorated his cheeks, he hadn't shaved in a couple of days but he made the rough look work for him. His thigh was pressed against her, and Hondo had moved from between them to sleeping on the other side of Brick—the canine's eyes were open and his ears flicked toward her.

She hadn't slept that well in a while, and she didn't attribute it to exhaustion. No, she'd been able to sleep because Brick had distracted her with his stories about dogs. Tempted to brush some of the hair away from his forehead, she settled for simply studying him. The man was attractive. It wasn't his looks that appealed to her, but his temperament and how he spoke. He didn't avoid difficult topics or shy away from unspoken desires.

Was he interested in her? Definitely. Did he ramp up pressure or press her for more? Nope. Instead, he'd held her hand and told her silly stories to make her laugh. He admitted to possessing flaws. Instead of playing tough guy, and pretending he could conquer anything, he accepted he had soul deep injuries and he'd learned to live with them.

Holding herself aloof from romantic entanglements wasn't new to her. An inability to be honest or commit to something long term while living a double life had become a fact. *But it's not anymore, is it?*

She'd walked away from the agency, and flown home. Her grandfather's cancer had been the excuse she needed to pull the rip cord on a life she hadn't wanted to lead anymore.

Pulling her attention from Brick, she stared at the ceiling again. Growing up in the circus had taught her a lot about self-reliance, the advantages gained through regular practice and hard work, and sometimes, the safety net wasn't a comment on ability but exactly that—a safety net.

Espionage hadn't been high on her list of life after college. She'd dreamed of something boring and stable—an office job. *Maybe secretary for a billionaire.* Her lips twitched at the idea. *Or a teacher or a tax accountant.* Her smile faded and she grimaced. Those jobs would have killed her. Not that they didn't have value, of course they did, but they weren't *her*. When the agency recruited her, she'd leapt at the idea and there'd been excitement. Most of the work was boring, but not all of it.

Years into the commitment, the need to keep her personal and professional lives separate had cut her off from friends, family, and even the promise of real romantic entanglements. Coming home had been her safety net and she'd fallen into it willingly. A glance to her left, she studied Brick's face again. On the other side of the safety net, he'd been waiting for her.

A chill raced over her arms as the moment the high-wire snapped beneath her echoed in her memory. She'd fallen, just as she'd always been trained, body relaxing as she tumbled through the air only to bounce on the net as it took the shock of her fall. When she'd rolled over, Brick had been right there.

Waiting.

A harsh exhale from the guy next to her and she frowned. His expression tensed. But his eyes remained lose. Hondo made a low sound and crawled up the bed on Brick's other side, and then pressed his head against his shoulder. Another bad dream, was it?

Taking her cue from the shepherd, she rolled onto her side and then curved herself against Brick. One leg over his, she just hugged him. No, she couldn't battle his demons away nor could she remove them, but she could be right there for him. A safety net, like he'd been for her.

Another ragged breath, and then Brick's arm came around her and she pressed her cheek to his chest. The race of his heart palpable beneath her ear, she let him catch his breath and kept her gaze on Hondo. As the canine relaxed, she began trace her fingers lightly along Brick's side. Contact, not tickling, had been her goal, but when he chuckled she had to smile.

"Good morning," he said slowly, his voice thick with sleep even as his heart began to slow to a regular rate.

"I think it's afternoon." The light slatting through the windows was bright.

"Well that's out there," he countered. "In here it's morning."

"Fair." She couldn't argue with the logic.

"How did you sleep?" He trailed his hand up her back until he cupped the back of her head. It created a cocooning effect, and she ignored the instinct warning her how close to the edge she'd drifted.

"Like a baby," she admitted. "Thank you for telling me stories until I drifted off."

"I'm glad, and I didn't take the snoring as a commentary on my ability to unravel a tale."

Pinching him, she grinned. "I don't snore."

"Are you throwing Hondo under the bus?" Playful challenge inhabited the words and she smiled wider.

The shepherd lifted his head at the sound of his name, and his mouth opened, tongue lolling out. "Don't listen to him, gorgeous." He rewarded her with a lick to her face and she laughed, a sound echoed by the man holding her. Lifting her head, she twisted to look down at him. "How are you doing?"

He combed his fingers through the wild curling mass her hair had become thanks to going to sleep with it wet. "Better every moment." His eyes were clear, and the firmness of his lower lip seemed perfectly edible. This was why she'd taken the job with the agency, why she'd sacrificed her time and her efforts— for moments like these. No one should ever be afraid or driven from their homes. If she could in some small part give back, she'd done that.

Now she was home and someone was driving her away from it.

"Someone just made a decision," he said softly, still petting her hair and she nodded slowly.

"I have. I spent years not being here...and by here I meant the states. I left my family, both the one I was born to and the one I grew up amongst. I kept myself on a short leash, and I avoided involvement." Admitting those facts were about her, not the job she'd done. "I did it all for the right reasons, and I devoted myself to them."

Funny, if he'd asked her the week before, she might have evinced some regret. Not this morning.

"I did what I had to do, and I think...no I know if I went back in time, even knowing what I know now, I'd do it all over again." She could own her choices. "Just like I know getting out when I did was also the right thing to do."

"Glad to hear it." He curled a lock of her hair around his finger. "But that's about decisions you made before, what one did you make now?"

"The circus is my home. I told myself the tour was so Granddad would rest and do what the doctors told him to do, but it's also so I could come home. Those people are my family, and I'm not going to hide away somewhere safe while they might be in danger."

He tugged the curl gently. "We're not one hundred percent certain the threat isn't directed at you, pretty lady. Leaving them may keep them safe."

"And it may not." No, she wouldn't second guess herself on this. "My gut says I need to be there. Whatever comes at them comes through me first."

A muscle ticked in his jaw, but all he said was, "I'm listening."

"If this is someone after me...you know...if it were after someone and they disappeared, I'd go after what they cared about to draw them out." It sounded kind of monstrous to say aloud.

"We've already established you went to the Darth Sidious school of getting things done." The light teasing note punctured her worry. He *was* listening. "It's a cold-blooded but effective method of getting what you want. They also wouldn't be the first to target innocents."

"Exactly. I know you wanted me out of there, and you were right saying maybe we could draw their attention off the circus, but I don't think it will work." Now came the hard part.

"You're going back." It wasn't a question.

"Yes," she confirmed. "I don't know who this is or why they want me, but unless we've found more evidence of who is doing it or what, then our best bet is to let me play bait."

He grimaced. "So far they've avoided direct confrontation, choosing traps instead."

"And they've missed…or at least not been as successful," she amended when he dropped his gaze to her bandaged arm. "Either way, I have to do this. I won't be the reason someone else is hurt. I've risked my life for duty, can I do anything less for family?"

"Not really keen on you playing hero," he said softly. "Or risking your life."

"Darling," she paused a moment on the nickname, then relaxed at his proprietorial grin. Fine, she'd go with it. "In the end, we all have to be our own hero, because everyone is trying to save themselves. I'm not asking you to do more than…"

"Hush," he said, silencing her with a finger to her lips. "You don't have to ask. Hondo and I will be there, but only if we have a plan."

Catching his finger, she kissed it. "Thank you."

"No thanks necessary, but I could use a favor."

"Name it."

"Move that luscious tush. You're both putting too much pressure on my bladder." The grumbled response made her laugh all over again, and she rolled off the bed. Hondo followed her and Brick shook his head. "See, we have to follow you."

"Oh?" She barely heard the statement as he stood, and stretched. She hadn't really been aware of the fact he'd only been in boxers and a white t-shirt when he came to bed. Probably should have, since she was also wearing one of his shirts, but damn—he looked really good all rumpled from sleep and just waking up.

"Yeah, my dog likes you even more than he likes me." Brick winked, and strode toward the bathroom. He even closed the door behind him, and she glanced at Hondo.

"Then I better not let either of you down, huh?"

Hondo didn't seem to mind one way or the other, but Wanda put her hands on her hips.

It was time to go to work.

They needed a plan.

DOWNSTAIRS, Brick turned her proposal over in his head. Despite what he'd told her, he really wasn't onboard with recklessly exposing her to someone who'd relied on sabotage.

"Maybe we're looking at it the wrong way," Jacko said via speakerphone. Jammer had been waiting for them downstairs, and after Brick let Hondo out to do his business and back in to eat, they'd fixed breakfast. Wanda pitched her idea to Jammer while they'd been cooking, but he'd neither approved nor dismissed the idea. "We're all trying to figure out if this is related to Wanda's not work with a not agency we don't need to name."

Brick didn't ask Jacko how he knew. In fact, it was his experience the less they knew about what the other man did in the name of investigation—the better. Wanda spared the phone a look, then raised her eyebrows at him. He shook his head at her unspoken question. He hadn't said a word to Jacko about Wanda's past, and he wouldn't. That didn't mean Jacko couldn't unseal files, and if he couldn't, well they had plenty of friends in and out of the field who could.

"We're assuming a lot about this, instead of looking at what we have." Unaware the eye play going on, Jacko pressed onwards. "Let's put the elephant sickness in the unrelated category, Wanda offered a convincing argument that animals get sick. We also talked to the vet on site and the vet in Vegas, both said the same thing. The elephant isn't that ill so much as they didn't want to add stress to an already uncomfortable situation."

"Scratch the elephant," Jammer said, loading bacon onto the three plates already over-flowing with scrambled eggs. Wanda popped toast out of the toaster and tossed them toward the men. They each caught their own and added them onto the plates as well.

"That leaves railway car vandalism. I'm putting that in the could be, but probably isn't category."

Again, Brick couldn't disagree with the information specialist. "Because as Wanda pointed out vandalism happens, it doesn't have to be related." At her grateful smile, he winked.

"Exactly, so if we disqualify those items and narrow it to just what's happened since they got to Eagle Rock, we can say—yes, there was a warning spelled in human blood left on the props trailer, some of the equipment was damaged—including Wanda's high-wire. Hey, someone get me a video of that, I managed to find some from a Bucharest show, but the quality isn't great."

Wanda's lips twitched. "Help us figure this out, and I'll send you tickets to see the show yourself."

"Excellent." Jacko's enthusiasm was contagious. "All I got out of Flint was more work, but for tickets to the circus, you get my above and beyond the call of duty work."

Smothering another smile, Brick crunched on the bacon.

"To that end, I've checked with the lab on the human blood tests—it's got preservatives in it, which means someone got it from a blood bank or other hospital facility. Creepy, but at least not from a body." Which would explain why no bodies turned up. "There were no prints on the sabotaged equipment, not that we expected them. Most of the workers use gloves when hauling and assembling, so they wouldn't even stand out. The other two pieces damaged, besides the highwire, were also not likely to hurt anyone, just break the machines down and prevent their use."

That was a relief, but it also narrowed their target to Wanda herself. Washing down his next bite of bacon with some coffee, he counseled his earlier patience and waited Jacko out.

"Finally, the big one—burning down the trailer. It was an incendiary device. Hank's people found it, and tore it down. Two interesting points, it had a timer on it and a receiver. They dropped it in the gas tank—so there were no explosives for Hondo to scent."

That chilled his blood, but Wanda looked at him questioningly. "That matters, because...?"

"A timer might have been set to detonate say in the darkest hours of the night, let's say 4 in the morning, when they could be sure you were asleep. The receiver though, was to detonate it whenever they wanted. Maybe they saw you on the move..." That took forethought and more than a hint of malice.

"...or they waited until we left to set it off.

Which means they are trying to hurt the circus and not just me."

"No," Jacko interrupted before Brick could respond. "I disagree. You are definitely the target, Wanda. Everything we know that was dangerous pinpointed *you*. That it didn't take place until you got to Eagle Rock suggests a narrower list of people involved, not a wider one."

"You think it's someone in the circus." Again, not a question, but it was Wanda who straightened as she spoke. "You think it's someone I know personally."

"Pretty much." Not the most tactful way Jacko could have said it. "Let's think for a moment, if Baz hadn't called your grandfather, and they hadn't brought in Hank's people... walk out the way events played. Some vandalism, then the bloody warning on the trailer. Then the fire which affected the two tents, possible accident but with everything else? We'll call it a test run. Then there's the accident with the high-wire—what if that hadn't happened until your opening night. The equipment malfunctions cause some stir. Those are all mishaps, but the warning was still there...

then the fire happens and you're killed or injured. The end result is the same, a misled investigation and a very seriously hurt Wanda, if not a dead one."

Brick suddenly hated the whole conversation. "Not pretty."

"Except I usually perform without a net."

Nope, Brick changed his mind. He loathed the conversation. "Do you have a death wish?"

"Not particularly," she snapped at him. "I've been doing this job for two decades, have some faith."

"I've got lots of faith, I also know when you play with a ticking bomb, sometimes you run out of time." He didn't mean to growl at her, but not even Hondo leaning against him soothed the naked fear racing through him at the thought of her high-wire snapping while she was up there without a net.

"Not that listening to you argue isn't fascinating, but could we get back to me?" Jacko interrupted. "Great. Whether the idea was to cripple you in a fall or a fire, the target is still you, Wanda. Which means getting rid of you was probably the goal all along."

Ignoring his food in favor of petting

Hondo, Brick wrestled his temper under control.

"Then my going back will piss them off big time." Beyond the grit and determination in her voice echoed a deeper emotion, a hurt and it evaporated his temper all at once.

"Hey," Brick said, reaching across the table, gratified when she took his hand without hesitation. "Whoever it is...they're the asshole. Only someone who didn't care about you could put together a cold, calculating plan to off you and make it look like someone just attacking the circus."

"An in*sidious* plan?" The quirk of humor softened the loss in her eyes.

"Exactly." He squeezed her fingers.

"Jammer, take a picture for me since they keep forgetting the important one is on the phone." Jacko's voice cut through the moment, and Brick chuckled even as Wanda gave the phone her middle finger. "Are we all listening to me again? Fantastic. The blood that was used, you know with preservatives? It's not just from a person. It was also mixed in with animal blood. So, Wanda, how close are you with the vet?"

"Frank? He's family. His parents have worked for my grandfather for years, we paid for his schooling and he came right back to join us. The animals are far too important to him...we all are." Then she paused.

"Except?" Jammer and Brick echoed each other, it was the first time Jammer truly joined in the conversation.

"Yes, except?" Jacko added when she didn't respond immediately. "The suspense is killing me."

"He's dating Lettie."

Before he could even ask who Lettie was, Jacko said, "Lettie Anderson, knife thrower— maybe an eight on the ten scale for hotness. The knives definitely add to the appeal. No record as an adult, sealed juvie record for...give the magic man a moment...for reckless endangerment and setting fires. Ding ding, I think we have a winner."

No, based on the shadow in Wanda's eyes, they didn't have a winner at all.

"Maybe we should call more people in," she said quietly. "Your friend, Cannon wasn't it?"

If she wanted to keep it all business, he would, for now. Brick snorted. "No, Cannon comes in like a wrecking ball. You've already had two fires." It worked enough to draw a hollow laugh from her.

"If it's Lettie, we have to catch her in the act. I don't know that I could believe it otherwise. And a juvie record," she said in the direction of the phone, "is sealed for a reason. I won't overlook the fact we have the information, but I don't see what she has to gain from getting rid of me or how I might have offended."

"Crazy doesn't need a reason," Jammer said solemnly.

No, it really didn't.

"Accepted. But the circus is my family, and I'm not abandoning any of them. We set a trap, and if we draw her out and she falls into it, then we deal with her then."

"I'm in," Jammer agreed, but Jacko remained silent. Probably waiting for the right moment to insert his trademark sarcasm.

"Sabotage is something I know," Wanda said, meeting Brick's gaze. She didn't shy away from the danger either, but she had come home for a reason. Someone was messing with her, and he didn't care for it. "I'm going to bet you know a lot about it, too. So let's think smarter, and not harder. If you wanted to get at me during the circus, how would you do it?"

He didn't miss a beat. "The high-wire."

"Exactly."

Hell. Crazy. Beautiful. Determined.

Mine.

Back to the circus it was.

CHAPTER 6

BY THE TIME they arrived back at the circus it was late afternoon and a line of vehicles and active midway promised a turnout. Wanda had called ahead, informing only Baz and Roger of what she planned. Brick had objected, but she remained adamant. Roger had watched her grow up, and he wasn't involved. If the guys wanted to keep an eye on him, she wouldn't stop them—but he would know she planned to walk the wire. Baz was also not on any list of suspects. He had every reason to keep her around to protect his cover.

When Brick and Jammer argued with her on that point, she'd called Ned Wagner. Neither man proved a fan of the intelligence officer, but they listened to him. Jacko had been even less thrilled when they alerted him to the Baz/Ned Wagner connection. Of course, his very cryptic, "Good to know. I'll make sure Flint is up to speed," hadn't made much sense, but she had to trust these guys.

They trusted Hank Patterson and his people —all of whom would be present tonight and she trusted them. Even as she got dressed in the red and white sparkling outfit she'd chosen for the night, she glanced at the trunk. She'd managed to save most of her costumes and items. She'd also gone through everything and double-checked her props. She didn't tend to use a lot but after the sabotage, it was better to be safe than sorry.

I do trust them. She trusted Brick most of all. Some time between his arrival with Hank's guys and curling up together the night before, she'd let him in. Most people described falling in love like a wham moment, a crackling, energetic fusion of two forces suddenly spinning together—drawn by gravity. But with Brick it was different…she hadn't needed a wham, they just blended and fell into sync.

Caring about him was as natural to her as

walking the wire, to the dance she did up there, and yet even thinking the word *love* was far scarier. He had the harder job tonight, all she had to do was perform—he had to watch her back from the ground.

Checking her appearance in the mirror, she repacked the trunk and locked it closed. A pair of rubber sandals over her nylon slippers would protect them until she was ready to climb the ladder. They'd installed a new wire, and she still needed to test it.

Outside the costume tent, Brick and Hondo stood waiting—and guarding. They hadn't wanted anyone to creep up on her while she was alone. He paused to give her the once over and whistled. "Damn, I thought the skinsuit you wore the other day was impressive."

Laughing, she did a little twirl. "People have to be able to see me up there." Rhinestones everywhere would glitter under the lights.

"I wouldn't miss you even in the dark," he promised and her heart did a funny little summersault. They didn't have time for that at the moment, so she leaned up to kiss him on the cheek.

"Good luck," she murmured, then gave

Hondo's head a rub. "Both of you. And you, keep an eye on the big man." She gave the last instruction to Hondo, and when her gaze tracked back to Brick's, she met his amused gaze. She didn't get more than a step before he tugged her back to him and then his mouth claimed hers.

The gentle massage of his lips against hers sent a wildfire response through her system. He didn't just kiss her, he teased, and tasted and then sought permission with his tongue for her to open to him. The contact couldn't have lasted long, and yet it was an eternity, just she and this man who took her breath away.

When he released her, a shudder rocked her system. Over stimulated and desperate for more, she raised her brows. "What was that for?"

"Tell me when we're done," he said with a grin and a wink. "You'll figure it out."

Lips still tingling, she nodded and headed for the Big Top. The show inside wouldn't begin for another couple of hours—but she wanted time to test the high-wire and any possible problems before a crowd was involved. Brick moved with her, but remained a few paces behind.

As he'd put it, he agreed to dangle her like bait but that didn't mean he was leaving her to dangle alone.

Inside, everything was set. The rings were in place, along with the grand stand. The new high-wire was up, and the flyers were locked up for now, but ready for release. A shiver chased along her spine, and her breathing deepened. Showtime demanded focus and preparation, a mindfulness of the moment in play.

Ascending the ladder, she was almost where she needed to be mentally when she stepped onto the platform and heard the click. A click that didn't belong.

Below, Hondo began to bark frenetically. Heart clenching, Wanda glanced down at her feet. All she could see was the platform. So what made the click?

"Don't move," Brick's voice reached her a moment before the man. "Do you hear me? Don't move."

This was her. Not moving.

A part of her didn't even want to breathe.

"Easy, sweetheart," Brick said as he reached the edge of the platform, though he didn't touch it. "I just need you to breathe and hold as still as you can."

"No problem." Bravado? Maybe. But she was almost to her happy place, she simply deepened her breathing and lifted her gaze. The wire stretched across from her platform to the other. Out there, on the wire—that was where she lived. Up here, away from all the noise and the distractions, she could just be. "Do I want to know?"

"Depends," Brick said, his tone almost conversational save for the undercurrent of tension.

"On?" Her weight was a little unevenly distributed between her left foot where it stood on the platform and her right, which was a half step forward. Not moving meant her legs began to burn from being held in the same position.

"How much you want to know." He'd disappeared from the periphery of her vision, but at least Hondo wasn't barking anymore. That was good, right?

"Let's say it's need to know, and I kind of

need to know. If I move so my right foot doesn't cramp, are we going to blow up?" He was right next to her, she did not want him hurt.

"At the moment, yes." A grunt strained out the last word. "Hang tight."

Okay. Maybe she hadn't wanted to know. A bomb. Someone put a bomb under the platform. Again, the only person coming up here would be her. The attack on her wasn't bothering her as much as *where* they chose to stage it. This was *her* space, her home, where she felt most alive and where apparently they wanted to kill her.

Movement across the line caught her attention. Someone else climbed the ladder on the other pole. But she could only see the flashes of motion, not who it was.

"Brick. How much longer?"

Was it Jammer? Hank?

Lettie?

Her stomach bottomed out at the last name. Lettie was a knife thrower, and a performer. She'd been with the circus awhile. Would she really turn on them? Her home?

"One more minute, sweetheart. Just

breathe. I need to block the pin, and you'll be good."

That meant nothing, but she would trust the confidence in his voice. Lettie appeared at the edge of the other platform, her head clearing it like some villain in the movie. The hate on her face though, even at this distance, struck like a physical blow.

"Almost there," he assured her, as Lettie made the last step onto her platform. She was dressed in her costume, all ready for the show. Knives sheathed in a belt she wore crisscross over her chest—something like a cross between a video game badass and a cartoon character.

It was the item in her right hand that held Wanda riveted.

The woman had a gun.

Where the hell was Jammer? Baz? The clowns! Anyone. Hadn't they noticed what was going on up here?

Of course they aren't, no one ever looks up.

The clowns truck was there, just beyond the other platform, but no clowns. Another click. "There," Brick exhaled, a shaky note in his voice. "I got it. You're good."

"Duck," she ordered, then ran across the

wire separating her from the other platform. She didn't slow, flowing from step to step aware of the weapon Lettie lifted. "No!" No one else would be hurt, no more damage would be done. She tackled Lettie right off the other platform, and they fell together—right into the air cushion inside the clown truck.

Lettie snarled at her as they bounced, but Wanda was used to riding the current and she regained her feet first. One solid punch—one that nearly dislocated her knuckles and crunched the bones in her nose—and Lettie went down.

Panting, she straightened and stared at the woman. Hopefully this was over—then she heard another click. "You should have stayed gone," Jojo said.

Really? Both of them?

Twisting, she found him standing a few feet away, gun trained on her. "No smart remarks? No more of your sarcasm?"

"My level of sarcasm depends on your level of stupid," she panted the words.

"I've got the gun on you, and you're calling *me* stupid?" Jojo's expression transformed to thunderous.

114

"Yep." She had nowhere to go, nowhere to hide and she faced him. Ironic, she escaped a bomb and survived a twenty-two foot fall with a crazy woman and now she was gonna get shot. If he wanted to shoot her, there was no way he was getting away with it. The threat to the circus would be over, though. That was the important part.

Incredulity filled his expression. "You're too stupid to even be afraid right now."

"No," she told him, lifting her chin. "Fearless doesn't mean stupid. Fearless means you trust the moment, you trust your skill, and you trust your friends."

He didn't get a chance to respond, not when a very large dog hit him at full speed. Hondo struck without warning and took his gun arm, a moment later Jammer was there and Hank, and everyone else.

They converged from all points, and Wanda walked over to the edge and found Brick waiting for her.

"Hi," she murmured. All of her calm seemed to flee, and her heart began to race. She'd run across the wire without a second thought for safety. Not when Lettie had a gun and she could have shot Brick. Taking the dive off the platform had been a calculated risk—but still a dangerous one. She'd been fine.

"Hey…"

"Watch it!"

"Wanda!"

The warnings came, but then so did what felt like a punch to her back, and the pain, which followed.

Somewhere, a gun went off—and so did two others.

Then she fell.

Hopefully there would be a net.

THE CHAIR next to the hospital bed was hard as hell on his ass, but Brick didn't care. The woman in the bed was all the reason he needed to stay right where he was. Hondo rested on the bed next to her. Three days since everything went to hell, but he hadn't moved. The staff had objected, but Hank put in a word and it seemed to carry a lot of weight with the staff.

Leaning forward, he took her hand. Someone—probably Roger—had stuck his head inside a few hours earlier to say her parents were on the way. Her brother was trying to get a flight from Europe, and her grandfather had called, twice. When her parents arrived, he'd given them a few minutes before they waved him back into the room. The whole circus was out in the waiting room, literally.

None of them had left.

"Jojo's in custody," he told her too still form. The bullet had pierced her right lung and broken two of her ribs. Thankfully it missed her spine, but she'd been in surgery for hours. Then they'd moved her to this room where he and Hondo had staked their claim. No way was he letting her out of his sight. "Lettie's dead. Your vet Frank has been cleared—we think he was another red herring. They planted a lot of them trying to make it seem like you *weren't* the target. The sheriff, Hank, and Jacko are all trying to sort out motives. I don't care, babe. I just care that they can't hurt you anymore."

Their trailer had been filled with a crazy stalker wall of info on Wanda, but then Ned Wagner had arrived and he'd asserted his authority in the investigation. It would be funny if it weren't a mess.

"Jammer's outside, he's got the door and plans to hold it in case they try to toss me and Hondo out again." Jammer had been the only thing keeping Brick from breaking a few arms when they'd tried to get him out earlier. "You know," he said, cradling her hand in his. "You were almost to the top when Hondo started barking. It's an alert, and I was moving. I left the SEALs because I damn near got my guys killed. Disarming explosives and scouting them...it's a game for the cool headed and steady fingered. I couldn't live with getting them killed."

He'd never admitted it aloud before. He'd known, even when he talked to the shrinks, he'd known. Didn't change that a mistake on his part nearly got them all killed.

"I left because I didn't think I had the nerves left for the job, but when you stepped on that pressure plate...nothing was going to stop me from saving you. I forgot to be afraid, I forgot to think about anything except getting you out of there safely." The corner of his mouth tugged upward. "What do you do? In my moment of amazing as Jacko would say? You one up me, racing across the wire as though you could run on air. I didn't even see that woman before you were running, and then when you tackled her."

His heart had stopped. All he could see was her plunging to her death and where was he? The wrong spot to help her.

"Then you bounced in that damn truck, and I was sliding down as fast I could." It had all happened so fast. "Jojo's never going to be able to use that arm again. Hondo got him good."

Blowing out a breath, he pulled her hand closer and kissed her fingers. "You saved my life, woman. You saved my life just by existing. I'd like very much to ask you out, but you're going to have to wake up so you can say yes."

His vision wavered, then her fingers curled against his palm and Hondo raised his head. Her lashes parted, revealing the most beautiful pair of brown eyes. "Are you okay?" The earlier intubation had left her voice rough, but he'd never heard a more beautiful sound.

"Hey," he whispered. "I'm fine, you know except for the being in the hospital because my girlfriend got shot."

"Oh, that must suck for you." There was almost a wheezing laugh, and he grinned before grabbing a cup with some ice water to hold to her lips. She took a drink, her eyes heavy. "Thanks."

"Anytime. How you feeling? Any pain? I can get the doc."

"I'm okay. You look like hell." She licked her lips, studying him. He hadn't left or showered in three days, but he would borrow hers in a few if it would make her happy. Hondo made a low sound, and she tried to move her hand. "Hey boy, thanks for the save."

The shepherd merely laid his head back down, not having to be reminded to be gentle with her. Her smile wavered, then closed her eyes again. "Tired."

"It's okay, I'll be here when you wake up." It was a promise.

"Brick?" Her eyes opened again.

"Yeah, sweetheart?"

"Girlfriend?"

He grinned slowly, his world righting with her awake and talking to him. "That's the plan."

"You sure? I'm a handful." The argument helped puncture the tension in his gut, and he chuckled.

"I can deal with it," he told her.

"Good." Then her eyes closed once more and she sighed. "I like to dance without a net, but you're a damn good net."

"You just try to get rid me," he challenged, but kept his voice low in case she'd finally made it back to sleep.

"Nope," she said, tightening her grip on his hand. "Mine."

Damn straight.

CHAPTER 7

ONE MONTH LATER...

WANDA SAT in the lawn chair, arms folded with Hondo at her side as Brick changed the tire on the truck. "You know I could help," she called. They were finally on the road to catch up with the Merry Circus tour—finally. A month post-surgery, and she moved slowly but she was healing. Regular exercise and lots of rest had been great for that, however, being babied was getting on her nerves.

"You're helping just by sitting there and being beautiful." Brick didn't even look in her direction when he said it.

Glancing at Hondo, she said, "Wanna go for a walk?" He was already on his feet before she stood. "Hey," she shaded her eyes and spotted ahead. "There's a campground down that way, we should go ahead and park for the night."

"We still have a few hours...or are you tired?" If not for the genuine worry in his tone, she might be aggravated.

"I'm fine, Brick. You change the tire then meet us down there," she said, pointing toward the campground. "Hondo and I are going to take a walk." Not waiting for his response, she set off. Understanding where his concern came from didn't make it any easier to cope with— he was afraid. Fear did terrible things to people. She considered all her options as she and Hondo followed the uneven land down toward the dip in the land where other trailers were parked.

It looked like the road did a switch back, they were somewhere in the mountains on their way towards a small town in western Colorado. She wasn't up to performing yet, she had at least another month before the doctors would give her clearance and then she'd have to start slow and build up her stamina. Two months off would take time to come back from much less after being shot in the back.

Thankfully, with all the witnesses, she wouldn't need to testify at Jojo's trial. There'd been talk he might be cutting a deal, and as long as the deal involved significant jail time, she was good with that. The past was the past, and she didn't pretend to understand the psychotic delusion the pair had shared. They'd even given it some weird name where the two fed off each other and she'd somehow become their target.

It sounded like a pile of BS, but then the government had taken Jojo into custody and Wanda had her suspicions. Today, none of that worried her as much as Brick's behavior. He'd been so great at the hospital and in the immediate aftermath. She'd wanted for nothing, but he wouldn't take the next step.

She was crazy for him. Nuts. In love. Weird words, but they all applied. The need to leap with him drove her every day, but Brick held back. First he attributed it to her wound, then to her stamina, and then because he didn't want to hurt her. Not that they'd talked about it in those terms specifically, but he eased away from kisses and halted it before they got to the good stuff.

"It's infuriating," she told Hondo, and blew out a breath as they reached the bottom. She was panting more than she should have, but she wasn't sure if that was from a physical or emotional cause. Hell, she was frustrated waiting for him to…

Maybe that was it. The high-wire wasn't for the faint of heart, and she'd always been perfectly ready to walk out, and dance on the line no matter what happened. Twisting, she glanced up the hill to see Brick had finished with the tire and was cleaning up.

They were going to camp here tonight. Just the two of them—well and Hondo, with her brand new trailer. *Our brand new trailer.* Decided, she pressed on and by the time he arrived, she was waiting.

"Let's get everything locked down for the night."

"Did you want to go get food?" There was the worry again. He was spending all of his time watching for landmines, and while she loved him for it—she needed him to be him again. He was so much more than her protector.

"We've got snacks. C'mon," she said, curving her finger to beckon him. Striding ahead, she entered the trailer and pointed Hondo toward the sofa. "Go take a nap bud."

He trotted off obediently, and she moved toward the big bed that took up a full third of the trailer. Since she had to buy a new one, she'd upgraded. So far, all they'd done was sleep in it. Today, that would change.

The door closed behind Brick and the latch dropped on the lock. Another thing she had to get used to, he locked doors behind them all the time now. He wanted to keep the world at arms length from her. If this persisted, her performing would make him crazy.

That would not do.

No sir, that would not do.

Toeing off her shoes, she nudged them aside before unbuttoning her shirt.

"Back bothering you?" Brick was there, his hands warm on her bare shoulders.

"Nope," she said over her shoulder even as

she unbuttoned her jeans. "You can do something for me."

"Name it." The adoration in his tone had her heart twisting. The man tied her up in knots in all the right ways.

"Get naked, please." She stepped away from him and tugged her jeans down. The bra and panties weren't exactly seductive lingerie, but they were more comfort than style. When she faced him, she found his gaze had gone hot and all her worries about pushing him went away.

Yeah, he still wanted her. Thank God.

"I don't want…"

"Ah." She held up a finger. "You say the words…hurt you…or strain you…or have you over do it, and we will have a fight. Got it?"

Brick considered her for a moment, then he stripped off his shirt, revealing rippling muscle and a taut build. Damn, that still did it for her.

"Better," she complimented him, then reached an arm behind her to free the bra and winced. *Dammit. Wrong arm.* Before she could switch, Brick was there, arms around her and then he released her bra for her. "Thank you."

"You're welcome," he whispered. Cupping

her jaw in his hand, he studied her. "Don't think for an instant getting you into bed hasn't been on my mind. I'm not a monk."

"You pretend real well..." She spread her hands against his chest. "I adore you for taking care of me. Love how you cherish me...but I need to be more than a fragile being you're protecting."

When he glided his hands down to her ass, and then lifted her, she locked her thighs to his hips. "Sweetheart, you're the reason I'm alive. Waiting a few months didn't bother me."

"Waiting a month has driven me crazy and you're thinking a few more?" It didn't come out a shriek, but damn close. The corners of his mouth curved and she growled. "Do you remember this?" Then she kissed him, the same way he'd kissed her that day. Only she didn't have to coax his lips to part, they opened to her.

Pivoting, he sat on the bed with her in his lap. His tongue tangled with hers, and he hand a hand in her hair and another wrapped around her, holding her steady and safe.

When she finally lifted her head, she met

his desire-filled gaze and smiled. "I figured out what it was for."

"Yeah?" He eased the bra straps down and she had to drop her arms to let them fall away, and then her breasts were pressed against his chest.

"You love me." Smug as hell, she grinned at him.

"Yes, ma'am." Then he pressed a kiss to the corner of her mouth. "You love me."

"Oh yeah," she exhaled the whisper. "I love you more than the high-wire."

"That's a hell of a compliment." He teased his fingers along the seam of her panties. She returned the favor, gliding her hands beneath the waistband of his jeans.

"It's a fact, and you're still wearing too many clothes."

"I have a feeling the minute these jeans come off, I'm not going to have the willpower to stop."

"Brick..." She bit back any angry or resentful words, and inhaled some patience. "The first time you kissed me, I couldn't stop thinking about it and then I stepped on a bomb that could have killed us both. You saved me."

"Then you saved me, yes, sweetheart. I was there."

Pressing two fingers to his lips, she silenced him. "Yes, you were. And the first time you saw me naked it was when you were having to help me shower, and use the restroom. Not exactly my finest hour."

His expression softened. "Seriously," he murmured, pulling her finger away. "You're a badass warrior, fearless, and true. You saved my life by more than taking that woman out. You saved my life by being you. Putting a leash on the need to have sex, a very small price to pay."

"Then unleash it, because I want you and the doctor told me a week ago that I was fine to resume normal activities." She'd used the word vigorous, but she didn't want to scare him off.

"On one condition." He tightened his grip on her before rising and turning to slowly set her on the bed. "If anything, and I mean anything feels wrong—you tell me." When he pressed her against the blanket then spread his hand against her abdomen everything in her melted. The desire in his gaze seemed matched only by the adoration in his voice. "I need to know it doesn't hurt, clear?"

"Crystal," she whispered. "Now get naked."

She didn't have to tell him twice. He stripped his boots, then his jeans, then returned to her on the bed. The first brush of his lips against hers and she was lost. Maybe she'd been fearless her whole life because really —she'd had nothing to lose until him.

WITH STEADY HANDS, he glided his fingers along her sides. Contrary to what she believed, seeing her naked while he'd had to help her shower during her recovery hadn't dimmed his need for her one bit. If anything, he wanted her more, loved her more. "You never give up," he said softly. "Have I mentioned how you saved me?"

"A lot," she replied, her voice a whisper. The ragged notes of emotion echoed his own.

"Good." As much as he wanted her, and as much as she wanted to push him to show it, he wouldn't allow anything to hurt her, least of all him. The skin around the exit wound was pink, and shiny. He checked it regularly, watching for signs of swelling or heat that might indicate infection.

Cupping her breast, he grinned at her sudden breath. Breathing had also been an issue, one she didn't often list when she recounted the different ways she'd improved. He knew the sound of every inhale and exhale she made. The short panting ones meant she couldn't get enough air. The first real, long exhale came out a relieved sigh. Then there were the ones in between...the ones where she worked on lung capacity.

"I'm not talking just about the dash across the wire." His heart might never recover from the way she'd rocketed toward danger. "I mean making me laugh in the dark." Gently, he caught her nipple between his teeth then sucked once. Her sharp inhale another reward. "How you challenged me with word games about the war between past and present...when you helped me see I don't regret my choices."

Freedom existed outside of regrets. Freedom to be himself again, warts and all as it were. Kissing a trail across her chest to her other breast, he savored the connect which seemed to fill him with every pulse of his heart.

Her skin was smooth in places, rough around the injuries, deeply tanned, and yet bright pink —comfortable and yet new. Beautiful, and strong.

Rising, he teased his way along her throat even as he dipped a hand down to her hip. "When you reminded me that life has to be fought for, and every moment savored." A gentle kiss to her earlobe, then a sigh as she began to free his jeans. "Even your impatience to capture the moment."

Laughter bubbled from her cementing the last way she'd saved him. "Are you seducing me or tickling me?"

"Neither," he promised, lifting his head to meet her gaze. "I'm loving you, every day, and I'm playing with you." He wanted to add for the rest of his life, but so much of who they were had been a rush through a collection of quiet moments. He wanted to take his time in every stage.

Then he kissed her, sinking into the feeling of the woman wrapping herself around him. One hand braced against the bed, he didn't let her bear his weight yet. A dance of touching, kissing, caressing, and teasing had him shaking before he took the time to strip away his jeans and claim a condom from his pocket. Despite what he'd said, he'd been ready for when she was.

Awareness of her injury ever present, he teased his way along her body, and then rolled them both onto their sides before settling her thigh against his hip. Gazes locked, he eased into her. The position forced him to go slow, to take his time even as it tested his control.

He hadn't let her down on that platform and he wouldn't now. Every stroke brought them closer and the world narrowed to the two of them. No words needed, they communicated through touch. She would hurry him, and he would slow her down. Demand became a gift, and patience a reward. When she came apart in his arms, he tumbled after.

On his back, he cradled her against him even as he played with the tangle of her hair. Moments like this were another part of the reason he loved her. She gave everything she was to what she did, she committed and pulled him into the dance. He wanted to be better for her, better for every experience.

"Clayton," she murmured against his chest.

She didn't call him that much, not since he'd asked her to call him Brick.

"Hmm?" He trailed a finger down her arm. He wanted to check her back, but it would spoil the moment. So he'd wait five minutes, then make sure he hadn't hurt her. Five minutes would be long enough.

"If that's you holding back, I can't wait to see what unleashed is going to feel like." The laughter trembling beneath the words belied the quiet aplomb of her tone.

A beat. "Is that a challenge?"

She lifted her head and her eyes seemed to dance as she looked at him. "Oh yeah."

Something settled in him, deep down where he'd held the part where he'd almost lost her too close. He'd fisted it, keeping his finger on the pressure trigger aware that at any moment she could slip through his fingers and be gone. Too many close calls, and then she'd been shot with him no more than a few feet away.

He wanted to keep her safe, a net against any future fall. To do that, he would have to clip her wings and that would be worse. Wrangling his Wanda meant letting her go, letting her be her and just loving her.

Committed, he spread his hand against her hip. "How's your back?"

"Wonderful," she whispered.

"Excellent." He rolled her over and just before his lips locked on hers, he whispered, "Challenge accepted."

EPILOGUE

JACKO DIDN'T EVEN HAVE to look at his watch. Ned Wagner appeared right on schedule. The parking lot was secure, but Jacko had friends and clearance. The lieutenant slowed a step, and then shook his head as he approached. "Of course you're here."

"You make someone under investigation disappear into a dark hole, be ready for someone to come looking with a flashlight." Jacko had always been protective of his friends, and even more so when innocents in the middle got caught in some game they were all playing.

"It's done," Ned told him, as calm and

unruffled as if he were discussing picking up a loaf of bread or buying a gallon of milk.

"Done done, as in it won't ever bite them in the ass again or done as in you're putting together a team to deal with the rest of it?" Retired or not, Jacko could smell an op five states away over the Internet. Ned Wagner had been making some moves lately, and this was the second time it involved a retired SEAL in Jacko's acquaintance.

The intelligence officer studied him, then raised his eyebrows. "Are you asking or volunteering?"

Adjusting his glasses, Jacko straightened. It wasn't finished...not yet. Hell yes, he wanted in. "When do we start?"

ALSO BY HEATHER LONG

Always a Marine Series

Once Her Man, Always Her Man

Retreat Hell! She Just Got Here

Tell It to the Marine

Proud to Serve Her

Her Marine

No Regrets, No Surrender

The Marine Cowboy

The Two and the Proud

A Marine and a Gentleman

Combat Barbie

Whiskey Tango Foxtrot

What Part of Marine Don't You Understand?

A Marine Affair

Marine Ever After

Marine in the Wind

Marine with Benefits

A Marine of Plenty

A Candle for a Marine

Marine under the Mistletoe

Have Yourself a Marine Christmas

Lest Old Marines Be Forgot

Her Marine Bodyguard

Bravo Team Wolf

When Danger Bites

Bitten Under Fire

Boomers

Yesterday's Heroes

The Judas Contact

Deadly Genesis

Unstoppable

Chance Monroe

Earth Witches Aren't Easy

Plan Witch from Out of Town

Bad Witch Rising

Elite Metal

Pure Copper (Elite Metal)

Target: Tungsten (Elite Ghosts)

Asset: Arsenic (Elite Elements)

Fevered Hearts

Marshal of Hel Dorado

Brave are the Lonely

Micah & Mrs. Miller

A Fistful of Dreams

Raising Kane

Wanted: Fevered or Alive

Wild and Fevered

The Quick & The Fevered

A Man Called Wyatt

Going Royal

Some Like It Royal

Some Like It Scandalous

Some Like It Deadly

Some Like it Secret

Some Like it Easy

Her Marine Prince

Blocked

Lone Star Leathernecks

Semper Fi Cowboy

As You Were Cowboy

Magic & Mayhem

The Witch Singer

Bridget's Witch's Diary

The Witched Away Bride

Every Witch Way But Floosey's

Mongrels

Mongrels, Mischief & Mayhem

Space Cowboy

Space Cowboy Survival Guide

Showdown at the Omega Kilo Space Station

Special Forces Operation Alpha/Brotherhood Protectors

Securing Arizona

Chasing Katie

Guarding Gertrude

Protecting Pilar

Wrangling Wanda

Shielding Shayna

Covering Coco

Wolves of Willow Bend

Wolf at Law

Wolf Bite

Caged Wolf

Wolf Claim

Wolf Next Door

Rogue Wolf

Bayou Wolf

Untamed Wolf

Wolf with Benefits

River Wolf

Single Wicked Wolf

Desert Wolf

Snow Wolf

Wolf on Board

Holly Jolly Wolf

Shadow Wolf

His Moonstruck Wolf

Thunder Wolf

Ghost Wolf

ABOUT HEATHER LONG

USA Today bestselling author, Heather Long, likes long walks in the park, science fiction, superheroes, Marines, and men who aren't douche bags. Her books are filled with heroes and heroines tangled in romance as hot as Texas summertime. From paranormal historical westerns to contemporary military romance, Heather might switch genres, but one thing is true in all of her stories—her characters drive the books. When she's not wrangling her menagerie of animals, she devotes her time to family and friends she considers family. She believes if you like your heroes so real you could lick the grit off their chest, and your heroines so likable, you're sure you've been friends with women just like them, you'll enjoy her worlds as much as she does.

Follow Heather

www.heatherlong.net

heather@heatherlong.net

ORIGINAL BROTHERHOOD PROTECTORS SERIES

BY ELLE JAMES

Brotherhood Protectors Series

Montana SEAL (#1)

Bride Protector SEAL (#2)

Montana D-Force (#3)

Cowboy D-Force (#4)

Montana Ranger (#5)

Montana Dog Soldier (#6)

Montana SEAL Daddy (#7)

Montana Ranger's Wedding Vow (#8)

Montana SEAL Undercover Daddy (#9)

Cape Code SEAL Rescue (#10)

Montana SEAL Friendly Fire (#11)

Montana SEAL's Bride (#12) TBD

Montana Rescue

Hot SEAL, Salty Dog

ABOUT ELLE JAMES

ELLE JAMES also writing as MYLA JACKSON is a *New York Times* and *USA Today* Bestselling author of books including cowboys, intrigues and paranormal adventures that keep her readers on the edges of their seats. With over eighty works in a variety of sub-genres and lengths she has published with Harlequin, Samhain, Ellora's Cave, Kensington, Cleis Press, and Avon. When she's not at her computer, she's traveling, snow skiing, boating, or riding her ATV, dreaming up new stories. Learn more about Elle James at www.elle-james.com

Website | Facebook | Twitter | GoodReads | Newsletter | BookBub | Amazon

Follow Elle!
www.ellejames.com
ellejames@ellejames.com

facebook.com/ellejamesauthor

twitter.com/ElleJamesAuthor